all tea, no shade, and a bit of murder

KNITTING, TEA, GOSSIP ... VENGEANCE

VIGILAUNTIE JUSTICE #2

ELLIOTT HAY

All Tea, No Shade, and a Bit of Murder (Vigilauntie Justice #2)

Knitting, tea, gossip ... vengeance

Print edition ISBN: 978-1-7397681-4-0

www.whitehartfiction.co.uk

Copyright © 2024 by Elliott Hay

All rights reserved.

No part of this book may be reproduced in any form or by any electronic or mechanical means, including information storage and retrieval systems, without written permission from the author, except for the use of brief quotations in a book review.

Most recent update: 24 February 2024

Editing by:

- Nicholas Taylor of Just Write Right
- Hannah McCall of Black Cat Editorial Services

Cover art by: Ilknur Mustu

❦ Created with Vellum

To the wonderful folks who bring you refugee-hosting programmes such as Room for Refugees and Refugees at Home. And to all the drag performers out there spreading joy and love despite the hate they receive in return.

content warnings

This work contains the following:

- People's lives torn apart by oppressive immigration/asylum systems
- Transphobia, queerphobia, and fear of drag
- Financial crime

The *Vigilauntie Justice* books are cosy(ish) noir(ish) stories set in London. They do have on-page violence, including murder, but it's never graphic. There's minimal swearing and romance and no sex – but there's heaps of queer content and found family.

author's note

This book is written in British English. If you're used to reading American English, some of the spelling and punctuation may seem unusual. I promise, it's totally safe.

This story also features a number of Canadianisms. Sadly, I cannot promise these are safe. You may find yourself involuntarily wearing a touque and craving Timbits and a double-double. It can't be helped. Seek treatment immediately.

Also, you may note that I capitalise both Black and White when they're used as race descriptors. Here's a handy explainer for why I choose to do so: instagram.com/reel/Cx8lsllqKk3

CHAPTER 1

in which madge & peggy have an argument

BAZ GRINNED as she switched off her mobility scooter and stood. Despite the chill in the January air, the sun was warm on her face. She nearly collided with two men walking down the street.

Letting out a small *meep*, she slapped her chest. 'Oh my. I'm so sorry, gentlemen.'

One of them, a rough-looking White man with a large mole just below his right ear, reached out to steady her. But when he caught her eye, he grimaced and withdrew his hand. The pair laughed harshly as they crossed the road away from her.

Baz shook her head – some people had no class. She stepped into the warmth of Wellbeloved Café. The familiar scent of coffee, pastries, and brown sugar filled her with warmth, lifting her mood.

'Morning, ladies.' Baz gave her friends a cheerful little wave as she stuck her head around the corner into the second room.

Only, the ladies weren't there. Or rather, Madge was but the others were missing. A man in Peggy's usual seat was in close conversation with Madge. Probably similar to their own age –

maybe mid-sixties. He had pale skin, grey hair, and what used to be called a weak chin.

'Oh, I'm sorry, Madge. I didn't realise you had ... well, that is ... I...' Baz didn't know where she was going with that sentence. She bit down on her lip as heat flushed her cheeks. 'I'll just go order my tea, shall I?'

Baz made to head to the front counter – only to run smack into Carole. Carole was a few inches shorter than Baz's five foot seven. But given how uncomfortably close they were in the moment, Baz could feel Carole's breath on her face. It smelt of bubblegum and ... pickles?

'Oh, Baz.' Carole grinned warmly. 'I've been meaning to tell you.'

Whatever incomprehensible bit of wisdom Carole had been about to impart was cut off when her... Girlfriend seemed the wrong word for a pair of septuagenarians. Wife – were they married? Baz couldn't believe she'd never thought to ask.

Partner. She'd heard Peggy refer to Carole as her partner before – hadn't she? Best to stick with that, then.

'Let the woman get her tea before you start filling her head with your latest theory, eh, my love?' Peggy winked at Baz as she steered Carole over to their usual seats.

Baz greeted the couple's Alsatian, Cookie, with a quick pat on the head as they passed.

Woman. It still made her heart soar whenever anyone called her a woman. She'd lived more than sixty years before she'd even acknowledged that truth to herself. But her new friends had only ever known her as Ms Barbara Spencer. Woman. One of the girls. A sense of peace blanketed her.

Baz turned towards the coffee shop's front counter. As she did so, she glanced at the artwork and handicrafts displayed on the shelves. Seeing a few of her own framed pieces of embroidery almost brought her to tears. She was so proud of how far she'd come since moving to London the year before.

'You're looking cheery this morning, Baz.' Sarah was Madge's youngest daughter and the manager of Wellbeloved Café. Her curly brown hair was pulled up off her face in a puffy ponytail. 'The usual?'

'What? Oh, yes. Thank you. I was just thinking...' Baz waved her previous thoughts away. 'Never mind. Oh my! What are these?' She waved at the plate of pastries next to the till.

Sarah grinned. 'Peach Danishes from Arapina, the bakery down by Trinity Laban. You're lucky we've still got any. Can I tempt you?'

Baz's mouth was beginning to water. 'They smell delicious. Yes, please.' She touched her phone to the reader to pay for her tea and treat.

'I'll bring everything over in a minute,' Sarah said. 'Let Peggy and Carole know I'll bring theirs too.'

Baz rejoined her friends in the next room – she'd all but forgotten about the mild-looking man with Madge. He'd vacated Peggy's chair and now stood behind and between Madge and Peggy, pointing over their shoulders at a light green paper on the table. Cookie was intently sniffing his shoes.

The man's voice was little more than a mumble, though, and Baz couldn't make out his words.

'Morning, ladies.' Baz took her seat in the corner. 'And, erm, gentleman.'

Madge looked up at her. Over the weekend, she'd changed her hair from a beautiful arrangement of braids to springy salt and pepper coils. 'I'm sorry, Baz. Have you met Arthur?'

'No, I've never had the pleasure,' Baz replied at the same time as Arthur said, 'Yes, we've met a few times.'

Baz's face flushed again. 'I'm sorry. Of course we've met. I remember now,' she lied. She didn't recall ever seeing this man before.

'Arthur's just been telling us about the council's plans for the nature reserve.' Peggy waved – her short fingernails painted bright blue – in the man's direction.

Madge looked at Baz. 'Arthur's the caretaker for a local nature reserve.'

Arthur pushed his glasses up. 'I also run the Facebook group. We've got almost 200 members. It's one of the largest groups in the area.' He shuffled his feet. 'Well, one of the largest *active* groups, that is. And certainly more than 100 members.' His voice was soft and he mumbled – but Baz was reasonably sure that was what he'd said.

Madge pulled her knitting from her bag and set to work. Peggy opened her laptop and set her fingers on the keys. Carole was already working on ... something. It would probably become another of the human bones or organs she created.

Cookie settled himself on the floor, curling up under the low table that stood between the women, still poking his nose out occasionally to sniff at the newcomer's shoes.

Arthur, clearly not picking up on the fact he'd been dismissed, muttered a few more words that Baz couldn't quite catch.

'Mmm hmm.' Madge didn't glance up at him. 'Why don't you do that on your way out?'

Arthur picked his mug and plate up off the table. He looked at Baz. 'Hope to see you there.' He muttered his goodbyes and crossed paths with Sarah bearing a tray of drinks and pastries.

Baz wasn't sure where or when he hoped to see her, so she simply smiled at him non-committally. To Sarah, she added, 'Thank you, dear.'

Carole began scooping spoonfuls of sugar into her cup

before pouring weak tea over the top. She picked up the small pot of oat milk and added the tiniest splash to her cup.

Baz preferred to let her own tea steep for a good long while before she touched it. She bent forwards to retrieve the paper the man had left on the table. 'What was all that about, then?' She read the photocopied notice.

Your cordially Invited to
The Friend's of the Bookmill nature Reserve
Extrodinrey general Meeting
Wednesday 24ⁿᵈ January
Don't let Them build over your Nature reserve!!!!!

Baz raised her freshly plucked eyebrows at his spelling and grammar. 'What's the Bookmill Nature Reserve?' She blinked. 'Oh, does he mean the park just to the south of me?'

Peggy rolled her eyes. Baz knew from experience Peggy could be a stickler for good grammar. 'Brookmill – not Bookmill. And no, you're thinking of Brookmill Park. The nature reserve is on the other side of the road, across from the south end of the park. Arthur says the council plans to sell the land off so it can be developed into flats.'

Madge studied her knitting for a moment. She sucked air through her teeth as she undid a few stitches before continuing. 'Lord knows we need more new housing around here.'

Peggy's trademark fuchsia hair was probably due for a dye as it had faded to more of a peach colour. 'I'll agree to the fact there's a need for more housing. But it absolutely doesn't need to be here. Green space is important.'

Pulling her glasses down her nose, Madge fixed Peggy with a glare. 'You see how crowded the neighbourhood is. Why don't we deserve new housing?'

Peggy lifted her right hand off her keyboard and shook a

finger at Madge. 'Don't give me that, Madge. Thatcher, may she rot in pieces, sold off all our council housing without replacing it. Of course we need new housing! This country is desperate for it. I never claimed otherwise. My point was that it doesn't need to be *here*. They should spread the load a bit.'

Baz gritted her teeth. She wished her friends wouldn't argue – it made her insides tie themselves in knots.

Madge's voice was warm and cordial but there was an undercurrent of steel and ice. 'I see. I wonder, what is it about our Black and ethnic minority community that makes you think we're not the ones who need this additional housing stock?'

Carole looked up from her handiwork and smiled brightly. 'Of course, they'll tell you it's a vegetable stock with scraps from the garden when we all know it's mostly made with the bones of displaced infants. It's why I never trust a vegetarian.'

In the four months Baz had known the women, she'd grown accustomed to Carole's interjections. Most of the time, her words meant nothing to anyone who didn't live inside her head. Half the time.

Peggy scowled. 'It's nothing to do with racism and you know it.'

Madge laid her knitting down in her lap – so much for Baz's hope this would be a brief argument. 'Shall I tell you what I see, Peggy? I see a middle-class White woman telling a working-class Black woman that our low-income neighbourhood doesn't deserve the investment of new developments.'

Peggy finally picked up her espresso and downed it in one. 'For starters, Madge, you're every bit as middle class as I am. Sitting there with your master's degree and your final-salary pension, lecturing me on...' She waved the rest of that sentence away with a flick of her hand. 'But more to the point, that's the opposite of what I'm saying.'

Madge poured herself a half cup of bright red tea from the thermal carafe she insisted it be served in. 'And what precisely are you saying?'

Setting the empty espresso mug down on the table, Peggy spoke slowly. It felt to Baz like she was choosing her words carefully. 'What I mean is that they've crowded us in like gherkins in a jar. And we all know it's *precisely* because this is a low-income neighbourhood. Surely it would be better to spread both people and new developments around more equally. The inner London boroughs have a population density of almost 12,000 people per square kilometre. It's barely a third of that in outer London. If we want to improve air quality, then we need green spaces. Why not throw up a tower block or twenty in Richmond or Kingston?'

Madge made a noise that might have been a chuckle. But before she could reply, the bell over the door sounded and a cheery voice greeted them. 'Yoo-hoo! Wagwan, ladies?'

CHAPTER 2

in which clive has something he needs to say

MADGE KISSED her teeth with a bit more vim and vigour than usual. 'Wagwan, Clive?'

Baz had been a bit perplexed the first time she'd heard the Jamaican greeting, but it was common in this part of south-east London and she'd grown used to it. Although she'd been born locally, she'd spent most of her life in Edmonton. Having been back for almost six months now – ever since her granddaughter had started at Goldsmiths, University of London – she'd already learnt to specify that she meant the Edmonton in Canada, not the one in north London, whenever she told anyone where she'd moved from.

Peggy's lip twitched. 'Say what you want, Clive.'

Baz was torn between her desire to get on with everyone she met and loyalty to her new friends. For reasons she wasn't entirely sure of, they despised Clive. He'd always been perfectly lovely to her. She'd never seen him do anything that explained their scorn. Nor had her friends offered up anything that led her to any greater clarity.

And yet they all loathed Clive – this small, slight, sixty-something Chinese-Jamaican man. Baz wasn't sure, but something about him seemed off today. She had to bite her lip to keep from asking him if everything was all right.

Carole faced him with a grin. 'Oh, Clive. I've been meaning to tell you...'

'Yes?'

'You know about the murder of Princess Diana, yes? Of course, everyone thinks it was carried out at the behest of Elton John.' Carole tapped the side of her head. 'But I know who's really behind it. You'll never guess.' She fixed him with a hard stare. 'Well? Go on ... guess!'

Clive touched his chest. 'Er, what?'

Oh dear.

Carole blew out a sharp breath. 'You're an idiot.' With a string of profanity-laced vitriol, she returned to her crochet. Baz was almost certain it was crochet.

Carole was quite happy to prattle on about her imaginary worlds and would tell you all about them. But she didn't tolerate being questioned. And she hated it if she thought people were humouring her.

Clive leant against Baz's chair, gently fingering the velvet fabric of the seat back.

She couldn't take it anymore. However much the women hated him – despite the fact that Madge sometimes slept with him – he was still a human being. And something was clearly weighing on his mind. 'Is everything all right, Clive?'

Madge pulled a face. 'Man's fine. He just wants attention is all.'

Clive straightened up. 'That's not true. I come here because the coffee is excellent. And because we're ... friends.'

'You're half right.' Peggy raised her empty mug and waved it at him. 'If you're not going to piss off already, make yourself useful and tell Sarah I'll have another when she's got a moment.'

Clive twisted his hands. 'We are friends, aren't we?'

Madge turned her head to look at Peggy, muttering, 'Oh, Lordy. Here we go.'

Baz's heart won out. 'Clive, you look peaky. I think you'd better sit down.' Grimacing at the pain that still bit into her when she put too much weight on her right knee, she fetched a chair from a nearby table. A knee injury had led to her retiring from the RCMP a few years early. She dragged it over next to her own, trying to position it so he didn't block the doorway from the café's main room. 'Madge, would you get him a glass of water, please?'

'Make it a soy latte.' A flash of Clive's customary haughty demeanour crossed his face for a moment. 'If you don't mind.'

'Of course. No problem at all.' But the look on Madge's face said she very much did mind.

Clive and Baz both took their respective seats.

Peggy lifted her espresso glass once again. 'Don't forget my espresso.'

Madge stopped midway through the entry in the thick wall between the café's two rooms. Touching the stone surface, she turned to face Peggy with a grin that was probably two-thirds syrup and one-third menace. 'Of course, my dear. Anyone else need anything while I'm up?'

Carole's attention briefly returned from wherever it had been as she faced Madge with a grin. 'Did you know that Gypsy Rose Lee, the American burlesque dancer, was one of Pope Geoff XIV's spies? She was tasked with identifying any Hittites in the population.'

Baz would've thought that was another of Carole's nonsense contributions but Madge nodded. 'And a pot of Rosie Lee. Anything for you, Baz? You know, since I'm being put to work.'

Baz felt a pang of guilt for sending her friend on an errand. 'No, thanks, Madge. I'm fine. But thank you.' She tried to show her gratitude through her smile.

When Madge headed off on her mission, Baz put a hand on Clive's arm. 'Something's bothering you, isn't it, Clive?'

He responded by laying his own hand over hers and gripping it with a ferocity that almost brought a tear to her eye. He blinked rapidly. 'He's gone!'

Cookie pulled himself out from under the low table on his elbows then stood up to his full height. He was large for a German shepherd but still not quite eye level with the seated Clive. Stretching his neck out, Cookie sniffed Clive before sitting down on the man's feet.

Clive buried his fingers in the dog's thick fur. He bent over Cookie's face and began to cry. Peggy glanced at Baz with an eyebrow arched.

'He's gone,' he repeated, though it was more of a wail this time.

'What do you mean? Who's gone?' Baz gently stroked his back.

Madge returned with a glass of water. She paused in front of Clive and held it out. 'Drink. You'll feel better.'

Clive looked up, tears still streaming down his age-spotted face. 'I said soy latte.'

Madge scowled as she returned to her chair. 'Good coffee isn't instant. Sarah will bring it when it's ready.'

Clive sniffed. 'Thank you. You're all very kind.' He drank most of the water before setting the glass on the table with a noisy clink.

Cookie crawled partway back under the table, only his large back end sticking out.

Madge and Peggy shared one of their glances then Peggy

looked at Baz and made a rolling gesture. *Get him talking*, Baz assumed.

Tears flowed freely down Clive's cheeks and his sobs were loud enough for everyone in the café to hear.

Baz's hand seemed to lift of its own volition. She hoped Peggy wasn't offended by the gesture.

Peggy rolled her eyes and then returned her focus to her laptop. Discovering that her crotchety, sarcastic lesbian friend was actually Trent Heston, a beloved author of sweet gay romance novels, had been a bit of a shock. Baz couldn't wait to tell her ex-husband that she knew his favourite author.

That is, she hoped to get back to a place of easy friendship with Hari where they could swap stories and trade gossip – though, as with any divorce, it would be a while before the hurt on both sides had healed.

Madge had retrieved her knitting project from her chair when she sat down and was hard at work. Or at least she seemed to be giving her best impression of doing so. Now that Baz was more familiar with her new friends, she could see that Madge's hands were moving more hesitantly than usual. She stopped to undo the last few stitches.

After a few minutes, Sarah walked in, carrying a tray of drinks. When she saw who was with them, she raised a questioning eyebrow at her mother. Madge responded with a subtle lift of her hand to indicate everything was fine.

Baz picked up Clive's coffee. 'Would you like sugar?'

'No.' Clive brushed his tears away with his sleeve. 'Thank you, Barbara. You're so kind.' He lifted the coffee to his lips and drank, then set it back on the table.

'Well?' Peggy's voice sounded strident even by what Baz had come to expect from her acerbic friend. 'Are you going to tell us what's brought on these theatrics?'

Clive sniffed. 'I'm trying to.'

'And for heaven's sake, man, speak plainly,' added Madge.

'It's Eddie.' Clive plucked a serviette from the table and dabbed at his eyes. 'He's gone.'

Madge kissed her teeth. 'Who is Eddie and where has he gone?'

Baz touched Clive's arm gently. 'Do you mean he broke up with you?' Despite his dalliances with Madge, she was reasonably sure he also liked men. Perhaps this Eddie had simply broken his heart.

'No, it's not like that.' Clive picked his coffee back up. 'Eddie is one of my flatmates. Blue rang me this morning as he hadn't shown up to rehearsal. She wanted to know if I'd seen him – and if not, could I fill in.'

Peggy drummed short, painted fingernails on the arm of her chair. 'I don't suppose asking you to tell this story in a manner that is both concise and coherent would achieve anything, would it?' She bent forwards, picked her espresso up off the table, and tossed it back.

'Sorry, sorry.' Clive set his mug on the table then sat up and took a deep breath. 'I live in a shared house with a bunch of people. One of the ones just off Edward Street, you know? There are six of us. It's nice. I mean, it's all right. Anyhow, Eddie and I both sometimes perform as part of Royal Tea. Have you seen any of our shows?' He looked up hopefully and smiled at the women.

Baz was curious what kind of performers they were. Musicians, maybe. Perhaps it was some sort of am-dram. Madge pulled her glasses down her nose and scowled at Clive.

Peggy made another rolling gesture. 'Skip to the end.'

Clive nodded. 'Eddie sometimes works at a pub over in Woolwich. Not every day, but when they ask him. He doesn't work the bar, of course; he's a cleaner. I do it too sometimes.

But Eddie missed two shifts last week already. And this morning, we were supposed to do our big shop.'

He for a breath. 'There's a cash and carry down in Charlton. We go together once a month to stock up. They have an excellent selection of Asian specialties as well as basic household supplies. We always go right after breakfast. Breakfast and then we catch the bus. The 177. Takes us right there.'

Peggy ran a wrinkled hand through her faded pink hair. 'Good God, man. We don't need a guide to the bus routes of south-east London. He's bunked off work and skipped out on a shopping trip. So what?'

Clive made a defensive gesture – though it turned into more of a pathetic wave. 'I haven't seen him since Sunday night. I went to the show. It was down in Catford last week. Did you see it?'

Madge scowled. 'For pity's sake! We're talking about one man who left the area – it's not as though there's a serial killer on the loose.'

'You think...' Clive blanched and Baz worried he might faint. 'You think he's been murdered?'

'When did I say that?' Madge kissed her teeth. 'I said nothing of the sort.'

Looking up from her computer, Peggy said, 'I'm still trying to figure out why you've confused us for the plod.'

'Filth!' shouted Carole without looking up from her handiwork.

Clive brushed a non-existent piece of lint off his trousers. 'Yes. Well. The thing is, you see...'

Peggy slammed her hands down on the arms of her chair. 'If you don't get to a point soon, Clive, it won't matter as we'll all be dead.'

He visibly bristled at Peggy's words – or perhaps at the snappish tone. 'I'm getting to it. You see, Eddie is ... well, his status in this country is tenuous. He applied for asylum several years ago. His claim was denied on the basis of a technicality. He was going to appeal but some of his documents were missing.'

'Mmm hmm. And you think the police won't take his disappearance seriously.' Madge frowned at her knitting.

Baz touched Clive's knee. 'The police have a responsibility to protect people regardless of their immigration status.'

Madge studied Baz. Peggy gave her a pointed look. Carole didn't look up but chuckled as she worked – though it was anyone's guess as to whether she was laughing at Baz's words or at something that existed in her mind only.

'My dear, you are lovely and kind.' Clive tittered, placing a hand to his chest. 'But you have a great deal more faith in the police than most people around here do.'

Madge breathed in slowly, like she was choosing her words with care. 'We all know the problems with the Met. I won't deny them. However, we also know there are good people working there, trying to drive change from within.'

She was incredibly proud of her grandson Peter, a local beat cop. 'If Eddie is really missing, then I agree with Baz that this is a matter for the police.'

'Hang on.' Clive sat bolt upright. 'What do you mean "if he really is missing"? You think I'm making this up? I can't believe you of all people don't trust me.' He got to his feet. 'I think I made a mistake coming here.'

Madge gripped Clive's arm. 'Oh, sit down. That's not what I meant.' Clive perched on the very edge of his chair.

Crossing her arms over her ample bosom, she added, 'I'm not suggesting you invented this story – only that...' She leant back, rounding her shoulders. 'These people, the ones let down by our immigration system... Lord knows there are enough of them. Their lives are precarious – their connections to society tenuous. Sometimes they just ... leave.'

Clive took a breath and opened his mouth but Madge raised a hand. 'Maybe he got wind of a raid in the works or he heard of a better job opportunity somewhere else. Perhaps he met someone or... I don't know. My point is that when people are unable to put down roots, it makes them feel less connected. It can prevent them from forming strong connections in the community.' She paused. 'And sometimes they just leave.'

Clive crossed his arms over his chest. 'He didn't leave. He wouldn't do that. *Something happened to him.*'

Madge shrugged. 'If you're sure of that, then you need to go to the police.'

Baz nodded.

A muscle in Clive's jaw twitched. 'I can't be the one to do that.' He stood back up again. 'I thought you ladies could help Eddie. Clearly, I was wrong.'

Leaning forwards in her seat, Peggy said, 'For pity's sake, Clive. If I wanted cryptic clues, I'd do the crossword. Explain what you mean. Clearly.'

'Well.' Clive's eyes darted over to Madge. 'I'm one of *those people.*'

Narrowing her eyes, Madge stopped knitting. 'What on earth are you talking about, you infuriating man? You're Windrush, just like me – are you not?'

Baz felt her breath catch in her throat. 'Surely you have every right to be here?'

She'd been learning about the Windrush Generation. After the Second World War, the British government gave all Commonwealth citizens the right to live and work in the UK. They later rescinded that right – but people already here were grandfathered in.

To think that she – who had lived forty years of her life away from the UK – had an inalienable right to be here, yet Clive, who had been here since childhood, may not... It really was despicable.

Clive pursed his lips. 'Yes ... and no. It's complicated.' He breathed out through his nose. 'I came here as a boy. All entirely legal. Went to school here. Completely above board. About twenty years ago, I lost my passport.'

Peggy made a puzzled face. 'So what?'

Clive offered a helpless sort of gesture. 'This was in the days before everything was recorded electronically, of course. Or rather, new passports were being tracked digitally, but they hadn't yet completed the digitisation of old ones. They couldn't find any record of my residency or citizenship.'

Madge furrowed her brow. 'And Jamaica?'

Clive laughed bitterly. 'It took a few years of chasing, but eventually the Jamaican authorities were able to provide me with a copy of my passport – last issued when I was nine. But, of course, all it shows is that I'm a citizen of Jamaica. There's no record of my travels or that I'd moved to the UK. In fact, it took quite a bit of effort to prove to the Jamaican authorities that I wasn't dead. They wouldn't take my word for it, you see.'

'What?' Baz wrinkled her nose. 'How is that possible? Surely they've got some record of you – some proof of your life here.'

Peggy and Madge both scoffed.

Clive studied Baz, his head tilted. 'I've been in south-east London most of my life – Brixton, Thamesmead, Peckham, Eltham. And a year ago I moved to Deptford. There's plenty of proof of my presence here. But there's no proof of my *right* to be here. When I moved to Deptford, it was because the Home Office found my last place. They were going to deport me. I got word of the raid and bailed before they could lock me up.' He shrugged.

'That's so unfair. I'm sorry.' Baz's jaw was so tight her words may not have been coherent.

Clive nodded at Baz then turned back to Peggy and Madge. 'You see now. I can't go to the police.' He shrugged. 'I don't believe they'll help. And if they do find Eddie, they'll just put him on a plane to Albania. Please, no police.' He grabbed Baz's hand and looked her in the eye. 'Promise me you won't tell the police.'

Bile rose in Baz's throat. 'I don't know.'

Peggy raised a hand. 'How about this? We'll take a look into it – speak to a few people and see what we can dig up. If we find anything suspicious, then we'll go to the police.'

Clive opened his mouth to speak but Peggy cut him off. 'I don't like you, Clive. Never have; never will. But that doesn't mean I want to see you deported. I wish you no harm. I'd be perfectly happy for you to live a perfectly happy life, so long as it didn't involve me. You and your friend don't deserve the harm the government is doing.'

'Mmm hmm.' Madge nodded. 'We'll see what we can find out. If – *if* – we get wind of any foul play, we'll discuss it with you before we go to the police. Assuming there's anything to go to the police with, that is. I still think it's more likely he just left the area of his own volition.'

Clive flapped his hands. 'Thank you, thank you.' He got up and ran to Madge. She swatted him away, so he turned to embrace Baz. Despite her misgivings, she hugged him back. Just because her friends didn't like him didn't mean she would be cruel to him. After a moment, he took a step towards Peggy.

Baz feared Peggy would throttle the man. But Cookie pulled himself out from under the table with a speed and grace that astonished Baz. He barked once – just once – but the authority in it was enough to make Clive apologise profusely.

Clive raised his hands, palms out, and backed away. 'You should come to the show tomorrow. Two o'clock at the community centre down in central Lewisham. I'll arrange tickets for you. You can meet everyone. Some of the regular guests too. And I'll talk to Blue – maybe we can chat afterwards.'

Madge nodded once. 'We'll be there.'

'Thank you.' Clive pursed his lips and made to leave, then paused. 'And thank you for the coffee.'

CHAPTER 3

wherein the ladies meet the queens

THE NEXT DAY, the women had a lovely lunch at Peggy and Carole's before heading out. Madge said she fancied the walk, so Peggy pulled her mobility scooter out from its parking spot under the communal stairwell.

The quickest way to Lewisham took them up Brookmill Road. Beneath her tartan coat, Peggy wore multiple layers to keep her warm despite the frigid temperatures. Her woolly hat had been crocheted for her by Carole. It was pale pink with a darker pink knobbly bit on the end. It amused her how people went out of their way to avoid saying it looked like a breast.

It did look like a breast. Peggy wore it proudly.

At one point, the pavement widened out a bit and Baz pulled her scooter alongside Peggy's. 'So where's this wildlife reserve that man was talking about, then?'

Peggy lifted her right arm and pointed. 'Just ahead on the right.' She still had no idea what kind of show they were due to attend. She hoped it wasn't music — she doubted there was a single musical act both she and Madge would tolerate.

Without slowing, Baz stretched her neck out to peer into

the middle distance. 'I've come this way a few times, heading to the big shopping centre — and I've never noticed anything on this side of the road.'

Peggy shook her head. 'You wouldn't. It's long and narrow and pretty well hidden behind the bus shelter.'

As they drew nearer, a hunched figure emerged from the reserve. With his hood up, it was impossible to be certain of his identity — though Peggy could guess. However much she agreed with Arthur's aims, the man could be a bit tedious. She didn't relish the idea of standing around in the cold, listening to him trying to persuade her of things she already knew.

Arthur secured the gate behind himself before turning to face the women. 'Ladies. Hello. What a nice surprise. I was just finishing up here. Have you, er, are you hoping for a tour? I suppose I could spare some time.' He fished a gargantuan set of keys from his coat pocket and moved to insert one back into the lock he'd just put in place.

Just ahead, a man emerged from the next street along, carrying what looked to Peggy's eyes like a protest sign. Although she couldn't make out the words from this distance, she wondered where he was heading. She loved nothing more than a good protest — she hoped it was a *good* one.

'What a lovely idea,' said Madge, striding purposefully up to Arthur. 'Unfortunately, we can't take you up on it today. We're on our way to a show.'

Both Madge and Baz being who they were, they stayed to chat in the cold. Peggy was frozen to the bone by the time the women got moving again ten minutes later.

Eventually, they arrived at the multicoloured building that housed the community centre. Angry shouting echoed off a host of surfaces. The closeness of the buildings made it impossible to tell where it was coming from.

As they rounded the corner, the small square in front of the building's entrance came into view. The ruckus was caused by a group of about eight or ten angry-looking White people – mostly men – stationed in front of the community centre. The man she'd seen emerging from the street near the nature reserve was there with his large protest sign. She was finally close enough to read it.

Teach our kids the ABCs – not the LGBTQs!

Peggy groaned. 'At least this lot can spell. That sets them ahead of many of their compatriots.'

She turned to check on Baz, unsure how she would cope with the sight. Her friend had pressed her lips so hard together they'd all but disappeared.

The protesters were chanting. 'It's okay to be straight. It's okay to be White.'

Oh, give me a break. Peggy shook her head.

One of the angry men carried an elderly boombox on his shoulder. The tinny speakers were pumping out that awful country song about small towns. As if they didn't know they were in the middle of London.

'Oh, Lordy,' Madge cried. 'What's all this nonsense?'

'Bunch of angry little men.' Peggy's fingers twitched. Part of her wanted to depress the scooter's accelerator, running down as many of them as she could.

But they had work to do. If she got arrested now, she'd miss the show – whatever it was. She eased off the accelerator as she steered past them, though she allowed herself the small comfort of extending a two-fingered salute. She made sure to look the pricks in the eye as she did so.

'Oi!' someone shouted. 'It's one of *them*.'

If Peggy thought the group was angry before, the roar that rang through them told her they'd barely started. But they'd picked the wrong little old lady to pick on. A growl began to work its way up through Peggy's core – she could take them all.

It took a moment to realise it wasn't her they were coming for. An icy chill ran down her spine that had nothing to do with the winter weather.

'Peggy,' Madge snarled. 'We need to get to Baz.'

A paunchy, grizzled man wearing a black T-shirt over dirty blue jeans was leading the charge. Despite his bushy beard, a brown mole was visible at the top of his mandible. Baz's face displayed sheer terror as the man and his acolytes converged on her.

Peggy's friend was an innocent – far from streetwise. Despite Baz's history with the Canadian police, she'd actually spent her career in a safe, clean office studying financial crimes. Even her time with Peggy, Madge, and Carole hadn't quite sullied her.

'You're one of them tr—'

Peggy put her thumb and middle finger into her mouth and cut off the bigot's speech with a whistle loud enough to get the attention of everyone in the vicinity. 'Oi, Basil Brush! Leave my friend alone, you great gammony lout.'

Baz's face quivered. She really was too gentle a soul for this nonsense.

Madge moved with surprising agility. She inserted her rotund form between Baz and the angry man. 'Young man, I know you didn't just mean to use that word. Because that word, I am informed, is offensive. And I know that you did not intend to offend my very dear friend.'

By this time, Peggy had caught up. 'You know what, dear. I think he did mean to cause offence. He's the sort who gets off on oppressing harmless little old ladies who don't have the strength to fight back.'

It was true – after a fashion. They couldn't take these guys in a physical fight. Maybe Carole could. She spent at least an hour a day in the gym, practising various martial arts and lifting weights.

'Ladies,' the angry man said, loud enough for everyone watching to hear. 'I think you need some new glasses. Your friend's a paedo.' His minions roared with laughter and cheered him on.

Peggy steered closer, bumping into him with the shopping basket at the front of her scooter and knocking him onto his arse. 'Oh dear. How clumsy of me. I really ought to learn to handle this thing. I didn't hurt you, did I?'

Several people hauled the angry man to his feet while an absolute brick wall of a man leant over Peggy on her scooter. A jolt of fear ran through her, tickling her toes. She glanced desperately around for Carole. Things were getting out of hand and she needed to—

'Gentlemen,' called a familiar voice at the same moment as Peggy spied Carole, her bag of knitting needles at the ready.

Peggy shot a glare at Carole, willing her to understand. *No.*

This situation was a tinderbox. Peggy wasn't sure how many hooligans Carole could take down before the rest of that group fought back. Madge could probably stop a couple of them with sheer force of will. But the only weapons Peggy had were words. And Baz didn't even have that – she could talk for hours. But her words weren't weapons.

'What's going on here?' Peter asked as he jogged towards them with his hand hovering over the baton London cops carried. His new partner wasn't far behind him.

'Old bat assaulted me,' the angry mole-man shouted, his finger stabbing in Peggy's direction. 'You all witnessed it, right?'

His friends chorused their agreement, crowding in around the four women. Someone in the group bellowed, 'She hit Mitch!'

'Young Peter,' said Madge indignantly. 'This ruffian here was being unkind to Ms Spencer. I stepped in to remind him of his manners. Ms Trent joined me in checking on our friend. Her sudden appearance must have startled him because he tripped over himself and landed on his bum.'

'She ploughed into me with her coffin dodger,' shouted the mole-man. Mitch, apparently.

Peter raised his hands. 'Everyone, please be quiet for a moment.' He glanced around the group, making brief eye contact with them all. 'Thank you for clarifying, G— good woman. Er, Mrs Dixon.'

The tips of Peter's brown ears flushed with colour as he turned to the mole-man. 'Now, Mitch is it?'

He grunted.

'Okay.' Peter held his hand out to Mitch in a placatory gesture. 'Now, Mitch. You're not hurt, so I suggest you and your friends move on over there, closer to the wall. Stop interfering with people's ability to access the community centre.'

'Not hurt?' Mitch pointed to his belt. 'Care to see the bruise on me arse?'

'No one wants to see your arse,' muttered Peggy.

Peter placed his fingers on the bridge of his nose and raised his other arm to indicate the direction the group should head in. 'C'mon, fellas. Right over that way. Follow PC Turner, if you would.'

When the group had moved on, Peter squeezed Baz's shoulder. 'You all right, Ms Spencer?'

Baz brushed tears from her eyes. 'Thank you, Peter. I'm fine.'

Peter looked towards his grandmother like he wasn't sure about that. 'I'm not sure what he said. But it sounds like it might have been a public order offence. If you want to make a formal statement, I can arrange that.'

Baz smiled. 'You're very sweet. Thank you. But I'd rather just go and enjoy the show if I may.'

Peter nodded. 'Okay. I'll see you ladies around. And, Granny, I'll see you on Sunday.' He waved and jogged after his partner.

Madge walked alongside Baz's mobility scooter and bent to envelop her friend in a hug. Carole appeared from nowhere and joined the pair, whispering words Peggy couldn't make out.

Peggy waited a moment then said, 'When you lot are done posing for the modern Norman Rockwell...' She waved her cane in the direction of the community centre.

Baz sniffed as her friends released her. 'Shall we?'

They made it the last few metres without incident. Baz looked at the angry crowd gathered on the far side of the square. 'Do you think our scooters are safe out here?'

Before Peggy could answer, a man exited the community centre and approached them. 'Are you here for the show? Who am I kidding – 'course you are. Come on in.' Baz looked like she was about to ask about the scooters but he waved. 'Bring the scooters. Plenty of space in here.'

Madge and Carole waited as Peggy and Baz steered through the wide sliding door. Baz thanked the man profusely.

He was short with heavily freckled skin and wearing a bow tie. Peggy guessed he was in his early sixties. His brown hair was close-cropped in tight curls. 'No worries, ladies. Normally, scooters are very safe outside. But that lot show up whenever we host Royal Tea shows. And, to be honest, I don't feel safe asking anyone to leave anything out there. Those chaps aren't very friendly to... I was going to say they weren't friendly to anyone – but they seem to like one another well enough. I suppose their anger's directed at anyone they see as *other*, if you follow me. By which I mean, please follow me.'

He set off across the floor, elbows rocking, swaying like a duck. After a moment, he paused and turned to face the four women. 'Oh dear. I'm so sorry. Where are my manners today? I'm Paul. Most of the time I work over at the library. But I also cover certain events here. Both run by the council, you see. We're in the Glass Studio today. Oh, actually... I've been assuming you're here for the show — are you here for the show?'

Madge stepped forwards. 'Good afternoon, Paul. Lovely to meet you. And yes, we are indeed here for the show. Clive said he'd leave tickets for us.' She shook the man's hand. 'I'm Margaret Dixon — but you can call me Madge. These ladies are my friends, Barbara Spencer, Peggy Trent, and— Where's Carole got to?'

Peggy tilted her head. 'You'll have to excuse Carole. I love the woman more than life itself, but one whiff of a table with tea and bickies and she'd sell her own grandkids.' Carole's yellow cardigan could be spied off in the distance.

'I see. Yes, I recognise your names. I can confirm there are indeed four tickets waiting for you. Well then, I suppose we ought to follow her.' The small man offered his elbow to Baz, who accepted, then sashayed in the direction Carole had gone in. 'Come on, ladies. We don't want to miss the start of the show.'

Peggy's hips were hurting her too much to move quickly — and Madge never moved rapidly. Or rather, not never, but never without good reason.

Still, they caught up with Paul and Baz just as they entered a light, airy space.

As Peggy followed, she asked, 'What kind of show will we be seeing? Clive neglected to mention.'

Without disrupting Baz's hold on his elbow, Paul clapped. 'Oh, you're in for such a treat, ladies. Blue's your host — as always. And today's guests are regulars to her shows. Di and Pfeff are familiar faces. Of course, Clive's usually in the audience but today we've got Coco on the roster. That's a last-minute swap, you understand. Might be different from the leaflet.'

None of that answered Peggy's question – but before she could ask again, she found herself facing a trestle table loaded with tea urns, a coffee percolator, and goodies.

Carole had a mug of tea and was heaping a plate with biscuits. 'People think that the Jaffa Cakes case was about tax, when in reality it was about the fact that oranges are part of their plot to cause congenital infertility. It took me ages to work it all out.' Having loaded up on bickies, she took Paul by the arm.

'What it really is...' Carole's voice faded as she steered him towards the seats.

Peggy chuckled to herself as she poured herself a cup of what was sure to be terrible coffee and put a couple of digestives onto a plate.

'Is he going to be all right?' Baz made a vague motion towards Paul and Carole. 'Should we explain about Carole's ... eccentricities?'

Madge waved a plate of biscuits dismissively. 'Don't you worry about Carole. She can take care of herself.' She poured a mug of tea from the urn.

Peggy doubted it was Carole that Baz was worried about, but she didn't say anything.

Once they had all fetched themselves refreshments, they carried their trays over to where Paul and Carole were sitting. The space was dotted with round tables, arranged such that they had chairs only on one side so everyone faced the stage, such as it was. There were dozens of people in the audience, mostly OAPs – though there were a few younger folks as well.

Paul looked up at them as they took their seats, a flirtatious glint in his eye. 'Ladies. Everyone find something to your liking? Sorry I got carried away listening to Carole. It's ... quite eye-opening, really.'

Baz pursed her lips, stifling a chuckle.

Peggy grasped Carole's hand protectively and smiled at Paul. His eyes followed her hand. She wouldn't tolerate anyone mocking Carole. Not that he was – just a proactive warning in case he was thinking of it.

Paul swallowed. 'Er... You ladies are in for a real treat today. Bluebird and Di always put on a fabulous show, of course. It's a shame Sue can't make it – she's such a laugh. Still, Coco is good fun too. And, as I say, Pfeff is a cracking performer.'

Madge took a sip of her tea and frowned slightly. She set the mug down. 'I'm still not clear, Paul. What kind of show is it we're here to see?'

Paul opened his mouth to reply before closing it again. Out the corner of her eye, Peggy spied a short man in a rumpled suit with a mop of wild white hair shuffling towards the stage. He mounted the single step and took hold of the podium at the front. She was about to suggest to Paul that one of the old dears had got himself a bit lost when Paul responded to Madge's question.

'Why, my dear, it's a drag show of course.'

The man at the podium faced away from the crowd for a few moments; he fluffed his hair and patted himself down before turning to face them. He set a few sheets of paper on the podium and tapped them before wiping his hands on his trousers as though the papers had been sticky, muttering to himself as the microphone kicked into life.

'Why is Boris Johnson here?' asked someone.

The man on stage looked up at the crowd and started as though he hadn't expected anyone to be present. He smiled –

awkwardly at first but rapidly gaining in charisma. The hair, Peggy now saw, wasn't white but pale blond. Despite herself, she found it difficult not to chuckle. It was a very good impression.

The man, who Peggy realised was actually a drag king, rested his elbows on the podium. 'Good morning, ladies, theydies, and gentlefolk. Ahem, ah, er... And, er, that is, it is Thursday afternoon. Or rather, er... As your Prime Minister, I've been invited here today—' It was, of course, Tuesday.

Paul cupped his hands to the side of his face and shouted, 'You're not the Prime Minister anymore, you blond twat.' Peggy joined the audience in heckling the performance.

'Ah, yes. Quite right. Er. Well, as I say, at any rate, I've been invited here today to welcome you to this, er...' He ran his finger down the length of the page. When he lifted his hand again, the page stuck to it. He crumpled it and tossed it aside. 'Er, as St Thomas Aquinas once famously said, carpe diem and welcome to the Glass Studio at the, er, one of the fine community centres in Lewisham. Ah, er...'

He ran a hand through his already mussed hair. 'Oh, yes, that's in London, I'm led to believe. My friend Lizzie lives just up the road over in Greenwich. Er, well, ipso facto, caveat emptor and at any rate she's not Prime Minister anymore either.'

'Too bloody right she's not,' hollered Peggy.

Madge glared at her for interrupting the show but at least a dozen other people in the audience booed loudly – it seemed to be expected.

After running his fingers through his hair yet again, the drag king rifled through his notes a bit. 'Er, yes, right. As I say, without going all the way ab initio as they say... I am De Pfeffel, your host. And today's spectacle for your viewing ... well, er, and listening, I suppose ... enjoyment is, ah, Royal Tea.'

A queen with a large blue wig done up in a 1940s style roughly shoved De Pfeffel aside. 'All right. That's enough from you, Mr Johnson.' She twirled around so everyone could admire her flower-printed dress with its full skirt. 'I am *actually* your host, Bluebird Sofa. And while we all know I'm the one you're here to see, we also have some excellent performers for you to look forward to.'

Bluebird waved at a plus-sized Black queen in a big blond wig. 'The lovely Shady Diana, Princess of Whales.' She put an emphasis on the H that left no ambiguity as to Wales the country or Whales the outsized ocean inhabitant. 'And lastly, we have a queen you may know. Give it up for Coco Celeste!'

The crowd broke into applause as the curtains at the edge of the theatre space parted and a petite queen in a red evening gown appeared.

Peggy almost knocked over her lousy coffee when Madge slapped her elbow, hissing, 'It's Clive!'

Peggy turned to her friend and glared. 'It's my hips that don't work properly anymore. My eyes are just fine. Better than yours, in point of fact.'

'JUST YOU WAIT AND SEE.' Bluebird held the final note of the song out for multiple heartbeats, betraying herself as a highly trained vocalist. 'Thank you, thank you. You've been a lovely audience. Thank you so much for joining us this afternoon. Next week you can catch us at drag bingo over in Bermondsey and the week after that we're in ... oh, I don't even remember. Be sure to grab a leaflet on your way out. They have all the details that I've forgotten.'

As the audience members shuffled out, a squealing, keening sound caught Peggy's ear. Within seconds Clive – or rather

Coco – pranced over to their table, squeaking with excitement. 'You came! I'm so glad you made it. I told Blue you were going to help. She's so pleased. Why don't you give us a bit of time to get changed? We'll join you as soon as we can.'

CHAPTER 4

in which it's never too late for a fresh start

THE WOMEN WAITED for the performers to join them, remaining in their seats after the other audience members had cleared out. Baz tried not to think about those horrible brutes outside. The things they'd said to her... The accusations they'd made. If it hadn't been for Madge, Peggy, and Carole, she probably would have gone straight home. She'd have spent the day crying, wondering if everyone thought such awful things about her.

But her friends had been fearless in their defence of her.

Peggy waved her hand in front of Baz's face, giving her a good fright. 'Yoo-hoo, Baz. Any chance you'll be joining us?'

Clutching her chest, Baz exhaled. 'Sorry, Peggy. Miles away.'

'And?' Peggy arched an eyebrow at her.

'And I promise I'm here now?' Baz replied, a bit confused as to what Peggy wanted her to say.

Peggy rolled her eyes. 'Oh for heaven's sake. It's normally Carole whose mind wanders off on us.'

'Oh, lordy.' Madge shook her head. 'What did you think of the show, Baz?'

Baz swallowed. 'Sorry, sorry. I thought it was wonderful. Don't you agree?'

'It was ... different,' said Madge. 'I've never seen anything like it. But very interesting.'

Just then, the door opened and a young woman with a messy blond pixie cut walked in. 'Ladies. Hey, hi. The fellows will be along in a moment. Takes me less time to get out of character than it does them. I hope you enjoyed our show.'

'If it isn't Alexander Boris de Pfeffel Oswald Ptolemy Chamberlain Ulysses Kemal Johnson,' said Carole.

The young woman grinned broadly as she raised her hands in surrender. 'You got me. Except, out of drag, I go by Alexa – because I'd rather not have people associate me with that odious man. Lovely to meet you all.'

'Likewise, Alexa.' Madge shook Alexa's hand. 'I'm Mrs Dixon. These are my friends, Ms Trent, Mrs Ballard, and Ms Spencer.'

Baz smiled warmly at the young woman. 'Pleased to meet you, Alexa. And you can call me Baz.'

Madge's eyebrow twitched. 'I will confess I am confused by all this. You appear to be – to my untrained eyes – a woman. Is that correct or am I just showing my ignorance? Apologies, I've learnt a lot about gender and sexuality in the last few years' – she waved towards Peggy, Carole, and Baz – 'but I still have a lot to learn. Are you a woman? And, I should be clear, I'm not asking what's in your pants, only how I should think of you.'

Madge had made a similar speech when Baz first met her. At first, Baz had been so humiliated by the question that she'd wanted to run from the room and cry. She was glad she hadn't done so.

Madge was a good woman. A *mostly* good woman – who sometimes did bad things. But only ever for good reasons. Just like the rest of their little group.

Alexa tried to hide a chuckle. 'I am indeed a woman. My drag persona, De Pfeffel, well... Pfeff's like a character I play. The other performers you saw today—'

The inner door swung open yet again and three men emerged. Clive was joined by a tall, chunky Black man of about forty or so and a slender White man who looked to be about the same age as Baz's friends – probably in his late sixties or early seventies.

'Wagwan, ladies?' The Black man touched Alexa's shoulder and flashed a charismatic smile.

Alexa touched the man's hand. 'I can't stay, unfortunately. I just wanted to spend a few minutes chatting with the ladies looking into Eddie's disappearance. And to thank you for your efforts. We all know how much the police will put into the disappearance of one asylum seeker. I'm just really grateful that someone is doing something.'

Clive accepted a hug from Alexa. 'I told you these ladies were the best – didn't I tell you that? They'll find Eddie – you'll see.' Still embracing the young woman, he turned to face the others. 'I can't stay either. But you ladies talk to Blue and Di.'

Madge raised an index finger. 'Now, Clive. We said we'd have a chat. If we agree to look into things, then we'll see what we can uncover. *If.* But we can't make your friend come back. He probably had his reasons for leaving.'

Clive shook his head vigorously. 'He wouldn't leave. I'm telling you.'

Alexa squeezed Clive's shoulder. 'It's okay. We'll figure something out.' Clive blinked back tears. They hugged the two other men before leaving.

'Ladies,' said the older man once Alexa and Clive were gone. 'I'm Keith – aka Bluebird Sofa. Most people just call me Blue but I'm not fussy. She/her pronouns if you'd be so kind.'

With a graceful flourish, she indicated her friend. 'And this is Ron – aka Shady Di.'

Ron nodded. 'You can call me Ron or Di, whatever tickles your fancy. Just so long as you don't call me late for dinner. Any pronouns are fine – I'm not fussed.' For such a big man, his voice was the same soft, melodic tinkle it had been when he was performing.

'Lovely to meet you both. I'm Peggy. This is my partner, Carole.'

'I'm known by many names,' said Carole with a cheerful grin. 'Atalanta, Teuta, Gudit, Lozen, Æthelflæd.' She tapped her nose. 'Some even call me Beatrix Kiddo.'

Blue blinked and opened her mouth as if to laugh before closing it again.

Baz leant across the table and offered her hand. 'I'm Barbara. Please call me Baz.' Introducing herself by her new chosen name still sent a little thrill through her every time she did it.

'And I am Mrs Margaret Dixon.' Madge folded her hands on the table in front of herself. 'You may call me Madge.'

Blue nodded. 'Clive said you'd help track down Sue Panova. Eddie. It's very kind of you to help. He's been missing the best part of a week now.'

Ron furrowed his brows, which had been shaved off and painted on. 'This isn't like Sue. I'm worried.'

Madge glanced over at Peggy and Baz before replying. 'We understand you're ... reluctant to go to the police on this matter.'

'Filth,' squawked Carole.

'Let's talk about that. We know Clive doesn't want to go to the police.' Peggy waved in the direction Clive had gone. 'What about you two?'

Blue licked her lips. 'They won't do nuffink.'

Ron touched Blue's shoulder gently. 'I trust Clive told you about Eddie's background.'

'We understand he's been let down by our immigration system,' said Peggy.

'That's putting it mildly.' Blue reached up and clasped Ron's hand. 'Clive said you'd travel with us back to Deptford. Would you prefer to walk or take the DLR? Either way, we can talk as we go.'

The four women looked at one another. Baz didn't mind – she and Peggy had their scooters, so it didn't make much difference to her.

Madge inhaled. 'Let's take the DLR. It'll be easier for you.' She pointed at Blue's left foot. 'If I'm not mistaken, you're suffering from Haglund's deformity. You really ought to reconsider your footwear choices.'

Blue blinked. 'Oh gosh. Someone's got a touch of clairvoyance! No wonder you're experts in finding missing people.'

Peggy cast a dark glare at Madge. 'Show off!' Turning back to Blue, she added. 'You'll have to excuse my friend. She's a retired nurse—'

'Nurse practitioner,' Madge corrected.

Peggy's eyes gave the merest hint of a roll. '—with a specialty in orthopaedics. Since retirement, she's reduced to making diagnoses as a party trick.'

'I see,' Blue said.

Peggy stood. 'Let's get a move on, then.'

The six of them bundled up and left the community centre together. Thankfully, there was no sign of the thugs from earlier.

The group made their way across the street to the station and to the platform. With the entire DLR network being step-free, Peggy and Baz were able to roll right onto the train without looking for an attendant to assist them. They were at the end of the line and there was still almost ten minutes before it was due to depart.

Ron and Madge followed Carole to the front of the train. The scooters had to stay in the open area nearer the doors, so the rest of the group remained there.

'I suppose you want to know more about Sue – sorry, Eddie. Edvin Marku.' Blue leant against the window next to the door. 'He hasn't told us all the details of his background but from what I've been able to piece together, he came to the UK from Albania to be with his husband around a decade ago. When that relationship ended, the Home Office advised him he had no option but to leave the UK.'

Blue's fair skin creased as she frowned. 'Since his move to London, his family had become aware of the fact Eddie was gay. It was a sore subject, but it was clear he felt like he couldn't go back. He said he'd have no life there.'

Baz nodded. 'How long have you known him?'

Blue made a graceful pirouette, dropping into a seat then pivoting back to face Baz and Peggy. 'Two years. That's how long he's been doing shows with us.' She studied her fingernails. 'The Royal Tea roster changes regularly. Di and I set it up back in...'

Blue looked up, as though searching her brain for the answer. 'It was 2018 – a year that you'd think would stand out in my memory. It's the same year Ron and I got married.'

Giving a little wave to her husband, Blue continued. 'Anyhow, when we first met Eddie, his asylum claim had been denied. They told him he hadn't provided enough evidence he was gay.' She raised both hands, imploring the universe to make sense. 'Evidence! The Home Office wanted proof of his gayness. I mean, can you even believe it?'

Peggy arched an eyebrow. 'I can believe it.'

'Yes, well.' Blue removed a water bottle from her large bag

and took a swig. 'Eddie got into drag as a desperate means of trying to prove himself to the Home Office. But once he started, it unlocked something inside him.'

She put the bottle away. 'That's what drag does. Creating a persona separate from your own is ... it's...' She waved a hand around like she was trying to pluck a word from the air. 'It's freeing. It's empowering. Emboldening – if that's a word.'

Baz nodded. 'It's true.'

Peggy leant back and studied her friend, the silent question visible in her eyes.

Biting back a smile, Baz bobbed her head. 'Yes. No. Not exactly.' All eyes were on her, so she elaborated. 'The first time I put on a dress was for a Hallowe'en party. I went as Jane Tennison.'

Peggy's eyes opened wide. 'Jane Tennison?'

Baz bit her lip. 'From *Prime Suspect*.'

The eyebrow climbed even further upwards. 'I know who Jane Tennison is. I'm just surprised at your choice of ... muse.'

'Anyways.' Baz wasn't sure what to make of that remark. 'It was just supposed to be for a party. A one-off performance. But I liked how it felt. I liked how *I* felt.'

'That's exactly what I meant.' Blue pointed in Baz's direction. 'Drag allows us to explore gender and sexuality stereotypes and cultural expectations. It lets us dig deeper into who we really are.' She bobbed her head a few times. 'Not that I've arrived at any answers, mind. But at least I've managed to have a few honest conversations with myself about who I am and who I'm not.'

Blue chuckled at her own words. 'Everyone should do drag at least once in their life. Did you know ... we actually go to nursing homes and retirement villages. Sometimes we perform like you saw today. But a couple of times a year, we spend a full day – doing drag makeovers for the residents. They're a big hit.'

Peggy nodded approvingly.

Baz found the idea adorable. She hoped she'd find something like that in her old age. Not that she was a spring chicken now. Her sixty-third birthday had passed a few weeks before. And her new friends were all older than she was.

'The thing is...' Blue shook her head. 'I've been out since the 1970s.'

'Likewise,' said Peggy.

'It was 1992 for me.' Baz ran a red fingernail down the sleeve of her cardigan. 'Or rather, that's when I acknowledged my *sexuality* to a few close friends. I...' Her breath caught in her throat. 'Well, I didn't come out as a woman until eighteen months ago.'

'Trust me, ducks,' Blue added. 'I am going somewhere with this – I promise.'

There was a soft jolt as the train began moving, pulling out of the station. The carriage filled with the grey light of day as the train emerged between rows of mid-rise buildings.

Blue took a deep breath before continuing. 'Then you'll both know what I mean when I say I've seen so many things, known so many people. I've loved some wonderful people over the years. Pretty much everyone I knew from back in the day is gone now. It sometimes feels like all the gay men our age are gone.'

The train followed the course of the Ravensbourne, a small tributary of the Thames that ran through south-east London. To the left of the train, the view was peaceful: trees and water. The view out the right featured an endless array of new-build flats.

Smoothing the legs of her trousers, Blue continued. 'Doing shows targeted at an older demographic allows me to ferret out the ones who survived by staying so deep in the closet that they were never at risk. Royal Tea's unstated mission statement is to make those folks feel safe and loved and accepted so they can finally acknowledge their true selves.'

Baz's heart warmed. A year ago, she'd still been living in Canada. Hari had just moved out of the house they'd shared for almost three decades. Her heart had been broken. And now... She was glad she'd taken the risk and moved to London with Daisy.

'Anyway.' Blue ran a finger along the back of the seat she was side-saddling. 'Once Eddie discovered drag, he came to work with us. He was planning to appeal his immigration case but, to be honest, I'm not entirely sure what came of it. He was working with a solicitor – I know that much. The Home Office lost some of the original documents he'd submitted with his earlier application. He'd been in legal limbo for a while, waiting and trying to gather all the evidence and supporting documents.'

The train pulled into Deptford Bridge station.

Blue gestured for the others to exit first. 'You may not know this but when I say legal limbo, that's exactly what it is. During the initial application process, the government provides some support for asylum seekers. Once an application is denied – even if it's on technical grounds, like you forgot to include one of your documents – that support comes to an end.'

The lift was too small for both scooters, so Peggy, Carole, and Ron took the first one.

As they waited for the lift to return, Blue added, 'Oh, you can appeal. But during the appeals process, individuals receive no support and they're prohibited from working. Unable to contribute, unable even to participate in society in many ways ... it takes a terrible toll on a person's mental health.' She shook her head.

Madge kissed her teeth. 'Believe me, I know. For the past

twelve years, I've been volunteering for a charity that houses people during that process. I've hosted a series of asylum seekers in my home.'

Baz did a double-take at that. *Had she really?* She knew Madge had lodgers – a lovely couple from Iran. And she'd previously had a young Ukrainian woman and her child. But Baz had assumed these were paying tenants.

'So you know that I am sympathetic to their cause.' Madge was holding up an index finger as if to forestall any argument. 'But what that also means is that I know how it goes. Because so many of the traditional means of building community are unavailable, they can find it hard to establish ties.'

The lift door slid open again and Baz wheeled in. The other two squeezed in after her.

Blue studied Madge. 'With all due respect, that's not fair. It isn't true.'

Madge glared up at Blue in the close confines of the lift. The two were polar opposites. Blue was tall, thin, fair, and almost gaunt, whereas Madge was short, rotund, and brown-skinned. But it was more than outward appearance. Blue was softly spoken – quiet but insistent. Madge was stern and sure of herself. She could be abrasive at times, but also quick to laugh.

In the cramped space of the lift, with its bare metal walls, the pair stared at one another. In the end it was Blue who caved first. 'I mean, it *can* be true. The system does make it hard for people to settle. But most asylum seekers work hard to build a community despite all that. They want to belong.'

Madge cocked her head and appeared to consider her words. 'Asylum seekers often lack the deep roots most people have. And the policies of this government have them living in fear.' She folded her hands in front of herself. 'A decade back, I had a man who stayed with me. Pius. A young man from Ghana. One day I woke up and he was gone.'

The lift door slid open at street level. Baz considered Madge's words. A soft rain had started to fall in the short time they'd been in the lift, so the group huddled beneath the overhead tracks.

Blue looked like she was going to say something, but Madge forestalled her. 'I'm not saying Pius didn't have his reasons. Lord knows that poor man had enough to deal with.' She stuffed her hands into her coat's large pockets. 'I thought something must have happened to him. I looked for him – I did. But it turned out he got a job in Liverpool and went for it.'

Blue frowned.

Madge sighed. 'Sometimes ... people just leave. It happens.'

Blue stretched a hand out and laid it gently on Madge's shoulder.

Madge smiled wistfully. 'He had my phone number and my address. If he wanted to get back in touch, he would have. A Christmas card might've been nice. Or even a phone call. But he was a very private man.'

'I'm sorry, Madge.' Blue gave Madge's shoulder a quick squeeze before removing her hand and clasping Ron's. 'That's not what happened to Eddie, though.'

Looking up at the concrete overhead, Ron said, 'Sure, sometimes queens leave the scene. Kelsey Preeze, Patsy Stoned, Fifi Galore. But they don't disappear entirely.'

'I think,' Peggy began, turning her scooter towards the main road, 'what Madge is trying to say is that we'll see what we can find out. But we can't promise anything.'

Carole walked to Ron and reached out towards him. When he raised one of his hands, she took it in both of hers. 'Thank you for dinner, Tiffany. I'm sorry about your cat.' She turned to Blue. 'And you... You keep building those Lego train sets.'

She blew a kiss at them as she left the station. 'Farewell. I don't think we shall meet again on this side of the veil.'

CHAPTER 5

wherein someone is sitting in peggy's chair ... again

WHEN THEY ARRIVED at Wellbeloved on Wednesday morning, Peggy found Arthur sitting in her chair. Again.

'Morning, Madge. Baz.' Peggy marched to her spot and allowed fat droplets of rain to drip onto his knees. 'Arthur.' His name came out as more of a growl than a greeting.

Here was this man, daring to sit in *her* seat. Despite the unsubtle hint, he still wasn't moving, so she thumped him in the shin with her cane and motioned for him to get out of her way.

'Sorry, sorry,' muttered Arthur. 'Morning, Peggy. Morning, Carole.' He pulled himself to his feet and waved at a stack of papers on Madge's lap. 'We've just been talking about the council's plans to raze the nature reserve to make way for a new housing development.'

Peggy squeezed past him. She hung her sodden coat on the back of her chair and lowered herself onto the seat. 'Disgraceful.'

He smacked his lips. 'Exactly.' He bent and tapped the clipboard Madge was holding. 'They reckon they can get almost fifty new units. Will you sign my petition?'

Peggy blinked. 'So many? But that nature reserve is tiny.'

Arthur snatched the plans from Madge and shoved them at Peggy. 'That space over up the top of Tanner's Hill – you know where the old traveller encampment was? That land isn't any bigger than the nature reserve. They put up more than sixty units – including some three-bed houses.'

Peggy scowled. 'Those eyesores blocked our sunlight when we were still living on the estate.'

Madge crossed her arms over her chest. 'I see. I thought it was about not overcrowding our community – not about some sort of architectural beauty contest. Hmmm?'

Peggy waved dismissively. 'Don't you start.'

'So we can count on your support for our campaign?' Arthur reached into his bag and pulled out a horrendously worded petition. 'The Friends of the Brookmill Nature Reserve is hosting an extraordinary general meeting over at the Baptist church in a couple weeks. We'll present our petition to the council then. Of course, if you'd be interested in supporting our committee, we could always use some assistance. Madge tells me you're a writer. Perhaps—'

Peggy fixed him with a glare and he shut up. Almost. 'I'll, er... I'll just leave you with a stash of petitions – shall I?' He pulled a stack of papers from his leather satchel and deposited them on Peggy's lap. 'Feel free to get them signed by as many people as possible. If you run out, just let me know. I've got more.' He stood up what probably passed for straight in some circles, smoothed his mousy grey hair, and departed.

'What a nice man,' said Baz.

Peggy shrugged and Madge harrumphed.

Baz pointed at the plate of pastries on the table. 'He bought us those.'

After unceremoniously dumping the petitions on the table, Peggy helped herself to a croissant. 'I suppose he can't be all bad, then.'

Madge shook her head. 'I don't know. That man has some wild ideas in the bedroom.'

Peggy bit back a chuckle as Baz was taken by a sudden coughing fit.

Madge continued undaunted. 'I don't mind a bit of play – you know, sexually. But there are some things a lady won't contemplate. Deeply disturbing proclivities. Unseemly.' She flicked her fingers as though some filth clung to them before leaning over her knitting to pick up a cinnamon roll.

Baz was still coughing.

Peggy touched Carole's knee. 'Would you get Baz some water, please, love? I'm worried she might never recover.'

'Of course.' Carole was on her feet in an instant. 'For drinking or bathing?'

'For drinking, please,' replied Peggy. 'Thank you.'

Carole disappeared through the doorway to the second room, returning a moment later with an entire ten-litre water dispenser in her strong arms.

Wordlessly, Baz held up her empty mug and Carole opened the water tap. Baz guzzled the water and thumped on her chest. 'Thank you. Thank you,' she spluttered. 'Sorry, I think some crumbs went down the wrong way.'

Carole proffered the water dispenser. 'More?'

Baz held her mug aloft. 'Please.'

Carole opened the tap again, letting water flow into Baz's mug until it reached the top lip. She shut the tap off without letting a single drop spill onto her friend's lap. Then she popped back through to the café's main room to return the dispenser.

Baz thumped her chest once more before taking another

sip. 'Thank you,' she said as Carole returned to her seat. 'That was very kind of you.'

The four women sat – only the ambient café noise, the sound of Cookie licking his paws, and the clacking of laptop keys and knitting needles disturbing the silence. Then a driver outside the window leant on his horn, slicing through the peace. This was followed by angry shouting.

'So,' said Madge at length.

'So,' replied Peggy.

Baz nodded.

Carole looked up from her needles. 'Of course, the pears won't be ripe until my grandchildren have grandchildren of their own. Mind you, I'm sure Diane was swapped as a child for one of those Greek replicas, so her grandchildren will most likely be maple trees.'

Madge set her knitting in her lap and bent forwards to pour another cup of ruby-coloured tea from her thermal carafe. 'What do we say? Are we going to help Clive and his friends?' She leant back in her chair and took a sip before smacking her lips. 'Mmm. Hotter than a witch's titty.'

Peggy waved a finger in Baz's direction. 'Might want to take a sip of that water before you start coughing again.' Madge sometimes spoke just to get a reaction – and Baz certainly made herself an easy target. Every blessed thing made the woman blush.

After taking a long drink of water, Baz set her mug down. She let out another small cough. 'Excuse me. Sorry. I think we have to – don't we? That is, I know none of you are especially fond of Clive but there's a big difference between being annoyed by someone and wishing harm on him – or his friends. And Blue and Ron were lovely, weren't they?'

'I suppose,' Madge conceded.

Peggy's lips twisted. 'You're right. I'm not sure I'd expend any energy helping Clive – but it sounds like this Eddie's done nothing wrong. I guess we should talk about where we start in the search for him.'

'Well, then.' Baz looked pleased. 'I, erm, I suppose I should fess up.'

Peggy arched an eyebrow.

Baz's skin pinked. 'I went on Royal Tea's website and downloaded a list of their forthcoming shows. I thought it might be useful for us to speak to a few of the fans. If we decided to help, that is. Sorry. I ... erm...'

Madge breathed out noisily. 'I called Clive and asked him to provide us with a list of Eddie's friends as well as the name of the pub where he'd been working. I've called them all already but no one had any useful information.'

'A tea party.' Carole's contribution to the conversation was so unexpected – not only because she didn't normally participate in planning their activities but also because of the mundanity of its content.

'What was that, love?' Peggy studied her partner.

'Tea.' Carole smiled. 'Emmy and Amrita will be joining us for tea and treats at eight o'clock this evening. I invited them.'

Baz frowned. 'Your neighbours?'

Madge narrowed her eyes. 'Does this have to do with Eddie?'

'Obviously.' Carole sighed melodramatically and rolled her eyes like a teenager.

Knitting needles still softly clacking, Madge leant forwards. 'Because...?'

Carole returned her focus to her knitting – but Peggy could take it from here. She could see what her partner was getting at. 'Because that pair know more about drag than we do. And because it turns out they've been to a few of Royal Tea's shows. We spoke briefly with Amrita yesterday afternoon when we picked Cookie up after the show. And because we know they'll be honest with us.' She touched Carole's knee. 'Good thinking, love.'

'Tea it is, then,' said Madge.

At a quarter to the hour, the entryphone buzzed. Madge, of course. Madge believed in punctuality – and according to the way she defined it, that meant being at least ten minutes early.

When Peggy opened the front door, she was met by Madge, who was pulling a wheeled shopping bag. 'Evening,' Peggy grunted. Cookie wagged his tail and barked excitedly.

'Peggy. And my sweet boy. Granny's got treats for you – yes, she does.' Madge petted Cookie's head before pulling her trolley into the flat. 'Come on, let's get this all set up.'

Peggy stood at the door, shaking her head for a moment after Cookie followed Madge through to the lounge-diner.

When Peggy followed a few seconds later, Madge was busy unloading multiple mismatched plastic containers of biscuits and finger sandwiches and cupcakes. She pulled out a small container and peeled the lid back. Cookie pulled himself into the prettiest sit, lifting his front paws up to his chest in almost a prayer-like pose. Madge handed him an apple wedge, which he crunched twice before swallowing. 'There's a good boy.'

Peggy stamped her cane on the floor – which didn't achieve much more than a dull thud on the carpet. 'Madge, what on God's green earth are you doing?'

Madge jabbed her fists into her hips as she stood up to her full five foot four. 'He likes apples.'

Peggy breathed slowly as she glared at Madge. 'That is not what I meant and you know it.'

Madge had the audacity to look surprised. 'What – this? We're having a tea party, are we not?'

Peggy frowned. 'You were *invited* to a tea party.'

'Yes.' Madge turned around and pulled more containers

from her shopping trolley-bag. 'My mama raised me to believe guests should never show up at someone's house empty-handed.' She reached in and removed a thermal flask.

Peggy peered into Madge's Mary Poppins bag. 'You do understand that Carole and I have also prepared for this evening, right?'

Madge studied her for a moment, her face impassive. 'What did you make?'

'I *can* cook, you know.' Peggy wasn't going to stand for this sort of insolence.

The eyebrow was still affixed in place. 'What did you make?'

Peggy's shoulders fell. 'I bought a couple packs of Ryvita.'

Madge resumed pulling lids off plastic containers. 'I'm sorry – I don't think I caught that. What was it you made for this evening?'

Peggy crossed her arms over her chest. 'I bought two packs of crispbreads. And a few cheeses.'

Madge tutted. 'Why don't you go into the kitchen and get some small plates, teacups, and saucers. You don't happen to have a sugar bowl, do you? And a small jug for milk?'

Peggy stomped off towards the kitchen like a disgruntled teenager. Before she got there, though, the entryphone sounded again. Putting her weight on her cane, she pivoted, heading to the front door instead. She buzzed Baz into the building and then opened the door – just as Emmy and Amrita were walking down the stairs. Baz walked in, carrying a large plastic container.

'Oh, not you too!'

Baz turned to look over her shoulder. 'Sorry? What?'

Peggy sighed. 'Come in, come in. Madge is in the dining room, prepping a feast for the ages.' She ushered the three new guests into the flat. 'You'll need to ask Madge what to do with whatever you've brought, as she's apparently running the kitchen this evening.'

Madge kissed her teeth. 'There is absolutely no need to be like that.' And then with no hint of shame, she added, 'Baz, you can place your tarts here next to my rum cake. I've sent Carole in search of a teapot. Peggy, where are you at with the milk and sugar?'

Grumbling under her breath, Peggy headed into the small kitchen – where Carole was about to put the freshly boiled kettle into the fridge. She took it from her and whispered, 'Go and have a seat – I'll be out in a sec.'

Keeping an eye on Madge through the open doorway, Peggy watched as her friend cast her eyes on the two young women, studying their empty hands. 'Good evening, girls. Ah. You've not brought anything. I suppose that's fine at any rate.'

Emmy smiled broadly – she really was an exceptionally pretty girl. 'Oh, not at all. We spent the afternoon making chutney.' She swung her shoulder bag down and reached inside. 'We brought a couple of jars. This one's mango and chilli. And this one' – she pulled a second jar from the bag – 'is cranberry and Prosecco.' She gave them both to Madge, before frowning.

Amrita stepped towards where Peggy was standing. 'Oh. We thought there'd be crackers and cheese. That's what, er... Peggy, do you want us to run over to Tesco?'

Peggy held the Ryvita and aged cheddar aloft. 'I think we're all good. We just need Madge to make some space for everything.'

'Ah,' said the woman in question. 'Peggy, will we be sitting at the dining table? I think we might be able to make space...' She began moving plates around in a futile exercise.

Peggy shook her head. 'I thought we'd load our plates up and then head over to the sofa. But what do I know? I only live here.'

PEGGY, Carole, and Baz sat on the sofa. The two young women were on dining room chairs dragged over to the coffee table. And Madge was on the armchair, keeping Cookie entertained with an endless supply of apple wedges.

'So,' said Emmy. 'Carole said you wanted to talk to us about the drag show you saw the other day?'

Madge nodded. 'That's right.'

Amrita swallowed a mouthful of crispbread with cheese and cranberry chutney before speaking. 'I don't really know what we can tell you ... but we're happy to try.'

Peggy brushed crumbs off her hands. 'Are you familiar with a queen called Sue Panova? She sometimes performs with Royal Tea?'

The two girls looked at one another. 'The name is familiar,' said Emmy.

Amrita frowned. 'We *might* have seen her. I'm not sure. What's she look like? What sort of act does she do?'

'Well, now.' Peggy cocked her head. 'That's the thing. We've only seen her on the website. The trouble is ... she's gone missing.'

'Wha?' Emmy covered her mouth as she swallowed a mouthful of cheese, cracker, and delicious homemade chutney. 'What do you mean *missing*?' Much as Peggy enjoyed Emmy's artlessness, she wouldn't endear herself to Madge with those manners.

Madge scowled. 'We mean what we say. Eddie... That is, Sue Panova... He... I mean she...' Scowling even harder, she waved dismissively. 'Eddie has gone missing. His friends have asked us to look into the matter to see if we can find him – or at least figure out where he's gone.'

'Oh my days,' Emmy said. 'We don't really know Eddie. At

all, I mean. We might've seen Sue perform – but we really only went to Royal Tea shows for Pfeff.'

Amrita added, 'We got into drag because of Alexa. She was in a couple of my classes last year. I'm doing anthropology – but I'm taking a few courses in theatre arts. Anyway, that's how we met them. We went to a couple of his shows and ended up getting completely hooked on drag as an art form.'

Madge looked like she was trying her best to hold back a lecture. Peggy suspected she was biting her tongue to keep from telling the girls they'd been no help at all – which, to be fair, was entirely true. Besides having a very nice tea party, thus far, the evening had been a waste.

Amrita took a bite of Madge's rum cake and practically swooned. 'Did you make this, Auntie?'

Madge helped herself to another slice of the same cake. 'I did.'

The girl swallowed another mouthful and wiped her mouth with her sleeve. 'This is even better than my nanna's. I mean, I wouldn't say that in front of her – not if I wanted to be invited to Easter dinner. But this is scrummy.'

'It's true.' Emmy nodded. 'I've had her grandmother's cake – and yours edges it. But they are both *so* good.'

'Thank you, girls. That's very kind.' Madge smiled. 'Now about this missing young man. You've seen some of Royal Tea's shows. And you might know some of the regular attendees, yes?'

The girls looked at one another. 'I mean...' Amrita frowned. 'We've been to a couple of their shows. But we don't know any of the performers – aside from Pfeff, obviously. And I'm not sure how we can help. Sorry, Aunties.'

'Obviously, if there's anything you need us to do...' Emmy helped herself to a slice of rum cake.

Amrita cocked her head and screwed up her eyes. 'Though

it is weird that there's *another* queer man missing in the neighbourhood – don't you think?'

Peggy's heart skipped a beat. 'How do you mean?'

Emmy studied her flatmate and then her eyes opened wide. 'Oh my days! You mean— Ugh, what was his name? William? Watson? No, Wilson!'

'I mean, okay,' Amrita began. 'It was a few years ago. But it's weird – don't you think?'

Emmy's brow furrowed. 'Yeah, I suppose. I think he was undocumented, so no one did anything.'

Both Baz and Madge were leaning forwards in their seats. 'What was that last bit?' Baz asked.

'Oh, sorry,' Amrita said. 'Undocumented. It means he wasn't in the UK legally.'

'We do know words, you know,' Peggy chided. 'I believe Baz was simply expressing surprise.'

Amrita's brown face flushed. 'Sorry, Peggy. I didn't mean—'

'Yes, yes.' Peggy made circling motions. 'Now, go on. Who is this Wilson and why is the case similar?'

Amrita spread some more of the mango chutney onto a cheese-crispbread stack. 'Okay, so. You know how we moved in here in August of 2021 – not long after you did, right?'

Peggy nodded.

'Our flat,' Amrita began. 'Apparently it had been sitting empty for a while. I mean, Tim, our landlord... He's not actually our landlord. I think he's, like, the caretaker or something. Whatever, he didn't think it was empty. He said the bloke was just avoiding him because he was behind on rent. I don't know if Tim got an order allowing him to enter the property or if he just went ahead and did it – Tim's a bit dodgy.'

'Well dodgy,' Emmy agreed.

Peggy was sympathetic – she'd had her share of shady landlords over the years. 'Ladies, if you don't get to the point soon, I'll be dead by the time you arrive at it.'

Amrita waved dismissively. 'Oh, please. You'll outlive us all, Peggy. But anyway, Tim said he'd give us a "deal" on our first month's rent if we cleaned up and packed away all the guy's stuff. Only some deal it turned out to be. We worked about twelve hours straight – d'you remember that, Ems? You, me, and Marlon. That's my brother. Anyhow, this deal worked out to less than three quid an hour for all the work we did.'

Madge sucked her teeth.

Amrita straightened up. 'Sorry, sorry. We had to bag his stuff up for Tim to put in storage. Wilson's stuff. But there was no way I was going to trust Tim with anything important, you know?'

Peggy made a show of checking her watch – not that she was actually wearing a watch.

'I know, I know. I'm getting there. It didn't look like Wilson had actually moved. He'd been food shopping – the fridge was full of spoilt milk and veg. We found his passport and a letter from the Home Office on the coffee table. I mean, not like we opened it or nuffink. It was already open.'

Emmy nodded. 'I only remember it 'cause it seemed so important. I think it said they were going to re-open his case.'

'Okay, you're going to think this is really naughty. 'Cause it is, right,' said Amrita.

'I know that *now*,' Emmy said. 'I'm almost done with my law degree.'

Amrita began tearing the wrapper off a cupcake. 'We kept it – the letter and his passport, I mean. Even then, I didn't trust Tim. I figured if the bloke came back, I could just claim I kept it by mistake. I kept it safe, though. It's been two and a half years, but if you think it could help, I'll get it for you.'

'That would be helpful,' Peggy said. 'Thank you.'

Baz – sweet innocent Baz – screwed up her face. 'One thing I still don't understand. You said he was queer. How could you tell?'

'Porn,' said every other woman in the room simultaneously.

Baz's face flushed to practically the hue of Madge's hibiscus tea. 'Oh.'

CHAPTER 6

in which unfair advantage is being taken

PEGGY ARRIVED at Wellbeloved armed with a full name, date of birth, and various other bits of knowledge gleaned from the passport and papers of the man whose flat Emmy and Amrita had moved into.

The only thing she was lacking was a chair. Hers was once again occupied. This time, Sarah was the interloper. Madge, Carole, and Peggy were Sarah's silent partners in the business. Hypothetically silent, at least. Peggy was reasonably certain Madge had more say in her daughter's running of things than Sarah would have wished.

Cookie made straight for Sarah, and sat on her feet, gazing up at her adoringly.

Sarah stroked the dog's tall ears. 'Morning, Aunties.' She pulled herself from the chair with the ease of youth. 'Sorry, I was just chatting with Mum about some childcare issues.'

Peggy squeezed past the woman to claim her seat. 'Is something wrong?'

Sarah waved the question away as she headed back to the café's main room. 'Ugh, don't get me started. I'll let Mum fill you in while I get your drinks. Morning, Ms Spencer.' Baz was just coming in the door. She greeted her friends before following Sarah to the front counter.

A few minutes later, as Baz settled in, Peggy turned to Madge. 'So what's got Sarah's knickers in a twist? Surely she can't think you object to an evening of looking after those boys of hers?'

Madge bent down to remove her knitting from its bag. As she sat back up, she shook her head. 'Of course not. I'd be happy to have them any evening. No, the trouble is with Henry's daycare.' She turned to Baz. 'That's Sarah's youngest. He's almost four. George is seven – he's in school full-time, of course. But Henry doesn't start until September.'

Peggy removed her computer from her bag and set it on her lap.

Madge untangled her yarn and picked up her needles. 'Henry goes to the local nursery, just around the corner from here. But when Sarah dropped him off this morning, the owner told her she's going to have to close up shop in a few weeks. The building's landlord is doubling their rent. Doubling it! Can you imagine? Disgusting. What kind of person throws babies out on the street? What a disgrace.' She sucked air through her teeth noisily.

Normally, Peggy found Madge's constant disapproval noises distracting and melodramatic. But in this instance, she was inclined to agree. 'That nursery's been there for more than a decade. All over south-east London, landlords are raising rents and forcing small, independent businesses out. It's unscrupulous. They won't be happy until every high street is identical to every other high street. A Tesco at one end, a Sainsbury's or an M&S at the other, with a load of betting shops in between.'

Sarah arrived and set the drinks tray on the table. 'Here you go, ladies.'

Peggy picked her espresso up and drained it in one go – without even pausing to savour the aroma. 'And only a Costa or a Starbucks for your coffee.' She slammed the cup back down.

Sarah sneered. 'Starbucks? You must be kidding. You wouldn't forsake my shop for one of the big chains, would you?'

Peggy wiped her lips with her fingers. 'Definitely not. No, we were just talking about this business with the nursery. It's not right.'

Baz shook her head. 'What a terrible business. I'm so sorry, Sarah.'

Sarah huffed and put her hands on her hips. 'It's unfair. Unfair to the kids whose routines will be interrupted. And to the parents who are suddenly going to have to scramble to find alternative arrangements. But especially unfair to Debs – she's worked so hard to build her business.' She pressed her lips together and inhaled before continuing. 'Can I ask you ladies a favour?'

Madge removed items from the tray and arranged them on the table, her wide sleeves in danger of being dipped into someone's tea. 'Of course we can look after young Henry. He'll be quite happy to play with his granny while you work.'

Sarah bent to pick the now-empty tray up from the table. 'Cheers, Mum. I'm grateful for that ... but it's not what I meant. I was actually hoping you could maybe help out the entire community.'

A barked laugh escaped Peggy. 'I'm not getting into the daycare business. Not my forte.'

Chuckling, Sarah shook her head. 'No, I suppose not. But that's not what I was getting at either. What I meant was... You ladies are... I don't know if you're aware of your reputation in this little corner of London.'

Baz swallowed as she looked up at Sarah, the colour draining from her face. 'Our what?'

Sarah laid a hand on Baz's shoulder. 'You wield a lot of power around here. Everyone respects you. People listen to you. When you ladies speak, people pay attention.'

Baz's shoulders rounded. 'Oh.' She breathed out slowly. 'That's certainly true. It's like I said when I first met you – you seemed like folks who looked out for your community. And even I, outsider that I am – or was, I suppose... Anyways, it was apparent even to me that you get things done.'

Peggy raised both eyebrows and looked pointedly at Baz. '*We* get things done.'

Baz nodded. 'You do. That's what I said.'

Peggy scowled. 'Oh for pity's sake, woman. You're one of us. *We* make things happen.' She drew a circle in the air, indicating all four of them. 'We. Us.'

Baz flushed. 'Oh.' But the very slight smile on her face spoke volumes.

Madge peered at her daughter over the top of her glasses. 'So what are you asking of us?'

Sarah shifted her weight from one foot to the other. 'I was hoping you'd have a word with the landlord? You could try getting them to see how important that daycare is to this community.'

Carole was studying a spot on her skirt. Peggy recalled the day she'd bought it. Carole said the floral pattern resembled blood spray.

'It wouldn't hurt to have a chat with the landlord,' Madge said. 'We can't promise they'll change their mind – but we can certainly try.'

Sarah's grin was infectious. 'Thank you.'

Her fingers continuing their work, Madge looked at her daughter. 'Leave the contact details and we'll have a word.'

Shaking her head, Sarah replied, 'Debs comes in for coffee most afternoons. I'll ask her to come and talk to you tomorrow morning if that works for her.' She turned to head back to the room, then stopped with a hand on the thick stone wall. 'Thanks, Mum. Aunties.'

As Sarah disappeared around the corner, Madge poured a steaming red fluid from her teapot into a china teacup. She leant back and took a sip. 'Now then. What have we learnt about this young man the girls mentioned last night – the second missing man in our community?'

One of Peggy's petty pleasures in life was in forcing Madge to wait. It was why she occasionally showed up a few minutes late to events. And this morning it was the reason she said, 'Were there homework assignments, Miss? Only I don't recall you assigning anything. Hang on, let's see.'

Peggy pursed her lips for a second before continuing. 'The girls told us about the young man who lived in their flat before them. And we had some crackers and cheese and a rather delicious chutney. Oh, and of course there was that rum cake you made. And the cupcakes. And the cucumber sandwiches. And the egg and cress sandwiches. And the doubles. And Baz brought some delicious Bakewell tartlets. In short, there was quite a lot of food. But I don't remember any homework, I'm afraid. Baz, do you recall Madge passing out any assignments last night?'

Madge sucked air through her teeth. 'If you are quite finished, Peggy.'

Baz looked like she was trying to stifle a chuckle. 'Actually. I did do a bit of digging, as it happens.' She clamped her mouth shut at a look from Madge. 'But I can wait to tell you what I learnt.'

Madge crossed her arms – the woman really did need to learn some patience. 'No, you go first. Please, I insist.' She glared at Peggy as she spoke.

Baz held a hand up almost in supplication. 'No, I'm sorry. I didn't mean to interrupt,' she said – which was patently ridiculous since she hadn't interrupted at all.

Madge held her mouth firmly shut.

Peggy exhaled noisily. 'Oh, go on, Madge. Don't get all het up. You know I can't resist teasing you sometimes. I promise I'm finished now. And Baz promises too – don't you, Baz?'

Baz zipped her mouth closed.

'Now.' Peggy arched an eyebrow. 'What did you learn about these missing men?'

Madge sat up straight and looked at both women in turn. After a few moments, apparently satisfied there would be no further interruptions, she said, 'I have a few connections in the immigration law community.' Peggy had to bite her tongue to keep from cutting Madge off once again to ask her how Chuk was. 'Now, no one I spoke to has heard of this young man – at least not based on what we learnt from Amrita.'

Madge took another sip of her tea then rested the china cup on her knee. 'But I did discover a few things. Firstly, most asylum seekers in this country are genuine and most claims are granted – eventually. The process isn't quick or simple but it does seem like they usually make the right decision. And in fact, most applications that are denied are due to technicalities. Insufficient paperwork or evidence or the applicant failing to understand one of the questions.'

Someone at another table dropped a crumb. Cookie appeared like a large, sable flash and snarfed it up – much to the surprise of the other patron. 'Oh my days! Where did you come from?' Cookie allowed himself to be patted for a few moments before returning to his spot under the table.

Peggy looked at the last words she'd typed in her newest novel. Will and Kitty were gazing at one another longingly on the banks of the Thames.

'Around half of applicants who appeal the initial decision

are ultimately successful,' Madge continued. 'Now this is where hosts like me come into play. This appeals process is torturously slow. That this man was able to rent an apartment of his own suggests he may have come to this country with significant resources. The process of applying for asylum and living here without being able to work is prohibitively expensive.'

Peggy was getting impatient. 'Yes, yes. We have a government of heartless bastards. We know this. Skip to something we don't know.'

Madge scowled. 'I'm setting the scene. My point is that it's not uncommon for people to vanish during the process. The fear of being deported sometimes overcomes the strength of the bonds people may have formed in their new communities.'

Peggy rolled her eyes as she returned her focus to her novel. None of this was new information. She flexed her fingers and began typing.

> Kitty looked up at the sky. 'Love doesn't see with the eyes, but with the mind. Why do you think Cupid's always painted blind?'
>
> Will crossed his arms, a cheeky smile tugging at his lips. 'That's very good, you know. I might borrow it.'

After a few tedious minutes, Madge arrived at something Peggy – who was only half listening – found marginally useful to their investigation. 'Once we have the young man's full details, my contact promised to check around and see if he can find out who was handling his case—'

'I can help with that,' Peggy said. 'I've got his papers. But we won't need Chuk to find out the name of the solicitor. I have that too.' She opened a very different file on her laptop.

Madge nodded. 'Excellent. What can you tell us about this man?'

Peggy squinted at the screen. She'd always had excellent eyesight – she'd never worn glasses and she certainly wasn't going to start now. 'Wilson Joseph. Born 1982 in Dominica. Worked for a local newspaper.'

Baz frowned. 'That doesn't explain his wealth.'

Peggy scoffed. 'Indeed. But it sounds like he came from money. And it does look like he's got good reason to fear returning home. Dominica is one of the last places in the Caribbean where homosexuality remains illegal. "Gross indecency" is punishable by up to twelve years in prison and, while the Prime Minister says they don't prosecute homosexual acts between consenting adults committed in private homes, there are no laws against discrimination or hate crimes.'

She shook her head. 'I found an article from the paper where Wilson worked, dated shortly after he left the country. They outed him and suggested he'd been trying to seduce a number of his colleagues to join him in his "wicked lifestyle". They even got a quote from his mother. Apparently, Wilson studied journalism and spent a semester abroad in Toronto. She said her son "turned gay" during his time in Canada due to "gay propaganda".'

Peggy bit her lip to keep from going off on a tangent. 'It's your fault, Baz. You and the rest of your countryfolk with your inclusivity and your tolerance.' The bitter tang in her mouth wasn't from her espresso.

Baz lifted her eyebrows. 'I wish I could say that everyone in Canada was so welcoming.'

After a few moments, Madge peered over her specs. 'And what about you, Baz? Did you do anything last night to further our investigations?'

'Last night? No.' Baz studied the work in her embroidery hoop before plunging her needle into place.

Although no discussions had taken place the night before as to who would do what or that there would be expectations on each woman to further the group's aims, Peggy knew Madge didn't look kindly on indolence. And, to be honest, she felt a twinge of disappointment that Baz wouldn't take it upon herself to at least undertake some research.

Baz looked up and smiled. 'No, I'm definitely more of an early bird than a night owl. I went straight to bed when I got home after our lovely tea party.' She pulled the needle back through the face of her embroidered scene. 'Of course, I did get straight onto the computer this morning to do a bit of digging.'

Peggy gave a sly smile. They'd chosen well when they'd welcomed Baz into their group.

'The land registry is a marvellous thing.' Baz sat up straighter. 'Did you know you can look up any property in this country to see when it last sold? And for a small fee, you can even check who currently owns it. All kinds of information is available.'

Madge looked up. 'I don't think every property is listed – only those that have sold since 1997.'

Baz's eyebrows raised briefly. 'Hmm. Interesting. Still... Now, sadly, you can't see tenant names – though I suppose that would be an invasion of privacy. But it is possible to view a history to see when a property has been listed for sale or to let. If it sells, you can see the date the sale closed and how much it sold for.'

Narrowing her eyes, Peggy leant forwards over the top of her computer screen. 'What property were you looking at? And, I'm curious, what were you hoping to find?'

Baz studied the scene outside the window for a moment,

watching the cars, vans, cyclists, and pedestrians passing by. 'I lay in bed for several hours, unable to fall asleep.'

She poured herself another cup of tea from the floral-patterned teapot and stirred in some oat milk. 'I knew you'd be counting on me to do my share of preparations and research. Peggy, you were the one with the details pertaining to this second missing young man. And Madge, if I live a thousand years, I can never hope to build the local network you have. You know everyone and everyone knows you. But just as I fell asleep, I thought about looking up the landlord.'

Baz shook her head and blew out a breath. 'But it was all for nothing. The flat is owned by an overseas corporation in the Seychelles – CCTM Holdings. I followed the trail for a while, trying to see if I could find where it leads, but it's a shell company – layers upon layers of useless information. I'm sorry, girls. I wanted to make a worthwhile contribution to the investigation and I spent two hours digging into it – but I came up with nothing useful.'

Peggy felt a flash of irritation. 'Stop that. This is not the time for a pity party. You researched a trail of evidence we wouldn't have considered. The fact it didn't lead anywhere is neither here nor there. It was a trail that was worth following.'

Madge nodded. 'You bring a different set of skills and a fresh perspective. And you're our friend. Peggy's right. Quit feeling sorry for yourself. We've got an investigation to get on with.'

CHAPTER 7

wherein someone makes a surprise visit

BY FRIDAY MORNING, the investigation into the two missing men had stalled. Baz had exhausted all the internet searches she could think of in relation to both Edvin Marku and Wilson Joseph. Peggy told her friends she'd continued to research the plight of asylum seekers in the UK. Madge was waiting to hear back from her mysterious sources in the legal world. And Carole ... was Carole.

Baz was reasonably confident Carole was crocheting today. She knew the other woman alternated between knitting and crocheting, though she still sometimes struggled to distinguish the two.

Baz's new embroidery pattern featured a snowy mountain scene that reminded her of Lake Louise in Canada. As happy as she was with her new life in London, part of her missed Alberta.

A stocky middle-aged Black woman stepped into Wellbeloved's second room and took a step towards the foursome. 'Good morning. I hope I'm not interrupting, Mrs Dixon.' She wore a long tunic with a lovely pattern in bold colours over burgundy leggings.

Madge paused her knitting – a beautiful ombre scarf – and looked up. 'Debs. How nice to see you. How are you?'

The woman smiled. 'Is now a convenient time for a quick chat?' When Madge nodded, Debs dragged a chair across from another table and perched on the edge of it.

'Ladies, this is Deborah Grant. She runs the Rise and Shine Day Nursery on New Cross Road. Debs, these are my friends, Ms Trent, Mrs Ballard, and Ms Spencer.' Madge indicated Peggy, Carole, and Baz in turn.

Madge seemed to be gradually placing slightly less emphasis on the *Ms* over the past few weeks – as though she were finally accepting it as a valid form of address.

'It's lovely to meet you, ladies.' Debs clutched a sturdy metal take-away mug of coffee to her chest. 'I believe Sarah told you about the problems I've been having with my landlord?' When the women said they had, she pressed on. 'I don't imagine there's anything that can be done, but – I don't know – Sarah seemed to think that you might be able to persuade them to change their mind about the increase.'

Baz looked at her friends before speaking. 'We'll never know unless we try.'

Madge's hands stopped moving as she studied the younger woman. 'Ms Spencer is right. You've worked hard to build your business. It isn't fair that someone should take it away from you. And you should do everything in your power to keep that from happening. If there's anything we can do to help, we'll be happy to do so.'

Debs' shoulders unclenched and her posture softened. 'It's hardly uncommon these days, though. I suppose I should be grateful I've had such a good run. Seventeen years I've been running my nursery in this neighbourhood.' She looked at Baz.

'Got started in my home when Lucy was small. She moved away to uni in Manchester just this past autumn.'

'How long have you been in your current facility?' Baz was the only one in the group new to the area.

'Oh, let's see.' Debs tapped her lip. 'It would've been 2012. We opened a couple of months before the Olympics. Before that, I had a much smaller premises a few doors down. Honestly, I'm starting to wish I'd never moved. It's more convenient for the parents and kids as the whole thing's on ground level and it's allowed me to expand and take on more kids and staff, but...'

She waved, as though wiping her words off an invisible blackboard. 'No, don't listen to me. I shouldn't be ungrateful. It's been a good run.'

Peggy inhaled sharply. 'You're allowed to be angry. This greedy so-and-so is trying to undo your hard work.'

Baz considered the situation for a moment. 'Can they even do that? Aren't there rules about how much they can increase your rent?'

Debs laughed. 'No, I mean, yes. Sort of.' She shook her head, her chin-length locs waving as she did so. 'During the term of the lease, they can't raise the rent except in exceptional circumstances. But when your lease is up, they can do whatever they can get away with. I was locked into a three-year lease – only it's coming up for renewal in about two months. I knew I'd be hit with an increase. But it's double!'

Her head fell forwards and she wrapped her hands around it. 'I signed the last lease in the middle of the pandemic. I wasn't even sure people were going to be needing childcare services in the same way as before Covid. I had a really good relationship with Brent, the landlord. He didn't raise my rent. But he died a couple months later and his kids sold the building. I knew I'd scored a bargain with what I was paying.'

Still hiding her face, she shook her head. 'I just can't do it. I'm barely scraping by as is. If my business goes under, I'll lose my house.'

Taking care not to put too much weight on her dodgy right knee, Baz pulled herself to a standing position and put her arms around Debs' shoulders. 'It'll be all right. You'll figure something out.' She looked over at her friends. 'We'll have a chat with your landlord.' When Peggy arched an eyebrow, Baz hastily added, 'And if that doesn't work, we'll help you come up with a plan.'

Baz wracked her brain trying to think what else they might do to help the poor woman. 'Perhaps I could take a look at your business plan and your accounts – maybe help you come up with ways to make your business more efficient. Erm, I'm an accountant, you know. Well, a forensic accountant. Retired. But I could try, at least.' She knew she was rambling but she felt like she had to offer something.

Debs brushed tears from her cheeks and smiled warmly at Baz. 'Thank you. That's very kind.' A perplexed look washed over her face. 'What's a forensic accountant? Sorry, I'm grateful for your offer – I'm just curious.'

Baz gave the younger woman's shoulder a squeeze and then returned to her chair. 'Forensic accounting's a sort of combination of accounting and investigation. We mainly look into financial crimes. So, in any given case, I might trace funds, identify assets, or perform due diligence reviews. It's a fascinating field, actually.'

Peggy arched both eyebrows. 'Fascinating? Ha! Frankly, I'd rather spend an evening with the Margaret Thatcher fan club.' She shrugged. 'No offence.'

Baz chuckled at Peggy's brusque manner.

Madge looked at Debs. 'And if your landlord won't change their mind, maybe we can find you a new property.'

'Madge knows everyone,' Baz said.

Debs took a long drink from her mug. 'I'm so grateful for your offer to help, ladies. Even if nothing comes of it. Honestly, that whole building is in such a terrible state of repair. I don't know how they can justify charging so much when they refuse to do any upkeep. Brent used to do what he could to fix things. But these new folks – they won't do anything. There's mould in the bathroom. There's a terrible draught coming in from one of the windows. And I'm locked in an endless battle with mice.'

She looked at her watch then hastily stood up. 'Would you look at the time? I told Jameel I'd only be gone fifteen minutes. Here's the caretaker's mobile number. It's all I've got I'm afraid. Thank you, ladies. Even if there's nothing you can do to affect the outcome, the fact you're willing to try is... I'm grateful.' She scribbled a number onto the back of a crumpled Tesco receipt from her pocket.

Debs waved and left the café. A few moments later, she could be seen running up the street towards the nursery.

The bell over the door sounded again. Baz couldn't control the warm smile that spread across her face as she glanced over. 'Paul!' After pulling herself to her feet again, she walked through to the shop's main room. A pleasant warmth spread inside her. 'How lovely to see you again.'

The bow-tie-wearing bespectacled man who'd sat with her at the Royal Tea show a few days ago gasped melodramatically. 'Baz? What on earth are you doing here?' He clutched his chest.

She nodded – feeling her own awkwardness as she did so. 'What brings you to ... erm ... sorry, that is, we don't often—' Good heavens! What was wrong with her brain this morning?

He straightened his already straight tie and ran a hand over his close-cropped curls as the awkward silence hung in the air.

'Sorry. Sorry.' Baz swallowed. 'It's a coffee shop. You've

come for coffee of course. And you're welcome to come as often or as little as you like. Just like all the patrons are.' And now she was blathering.

Paul was handsome in an eccentric sort of way: small and slight with the barest hint of a moustache. He glanced around in an exaggerated fashion. 'Do you know? I've never spotted this place? I don't live far – only over on the estate. The one by the leisure centre, I mean. But it's just off the main road and I've never noticed it before, innit? I, er, I was out for a walk this morning, letting my feet carry me where they would. And, wouldn't you know it, they led me to you. What a coincidence!'

Baz touched her ear but couldn't think of what to say.

Paul studied his shoes as though he thought perhaps they were to blame for bringing him here. 'So, er...' He tugged on his ear. 'Do you come here often?'

'Oh, yes,' Baz said. 'My friends and I meet here every morning. We drink our tea, do some crafting, and have a bit of a chat.' She motioned towards the second room, where her friends were silently watching Baz's exchange with Paul. Madge gave a small wave.

Baz felt her skin flush. The curse of being a ginger.

'It's Paul, isn't it?' asked Peggy.

'Oh my! You're all here.' The dapper man stepped through the open doorway to the second room. 'And yes, it is. Good morning, ladies. How lovely to see you.' He straightened his bow tie again. 'Let's see if I've got this straight... Madge, Carole, and Peg.'

'It's Peggy – never Peg.' Peggy tapped her electric blue fingernails on the arms of her chair. 'And she's me. That's Carole.' She indicated her partner – the one Paul had called Peg.

Carole looked up and smiled as she nodded at Paul. 'How delightful to meet you. I was an anthropologist who married a farmer in Gambia. During our life there, I learnt to hunt and fight. When my husband was killed, I returned to London to earn a PhD in anthropology. I was the curator of the British museum when I first encountered Peggy.'

Paul raised a finger and made to point it, then seemed to change his mind and curled it back in. He frowned but then a grin spread across his face. '*The Avengers?*'

Carole sneered. 'Don't be ludicrous.'

He narrowed his eyes. 'That was Cathy Gale's biography.'

Carole shrugged and returned her focus to her crochet work – a pair of life-sized human lungs. 'They had to get their ideas from somewhere.'

Peggy fixed him with one of her stares, eyebrows slightly raised as though daring him to challenge her partner's sanity.

Paul opened his mouth, then closed it again.

Baz fought to regain some semblance of peace and predictability in her morning. 'Girls, you remember Paul, don't you? He works at the community centre – we met him at the show a few days ago.'

Madge patted the seat so recently vacated by Debs. 'Good to see you again, Paul. Take a seat.' Her tone made it clear this wasn't a request.

Paul sat and crossed his legs. 'My, my. What a lovely place this is. Has it been here long?'

'Thank you. It's been open for two and a half years.' Madge peered over the top of her glasses. 'Now, young man, as you may be aware, one of Royal Tea's, ah, performers...' She turned to Peggy. 'Is that the right term?'

When Peggy assented, Madge continued. 'One of their performers has recently gone missing. The others have asked us to look into the matter – to see if we can uncover what happened to...' She looked at Peggy again. 'Is "her" the correct pronoun here?'

'Madge, it's the person we're looking for, not the queen. As we have all repeatedly heard over the past few days, Eddie uses he/him pronouns.' Peggy's eyes never left her computer screen.

'I don't want to get it wrong, do I?' Madge looked back at Paul. 'As I said, they've asked us to see if we can uncover what happened to Eddie. Now, do you attend many of Royal Tea's shows?'

'A mystery!' Paul's eyes were wide as he brought his hands together. 'My, how fascinating. And, yes, I do, as a matter of fact. I'm a regular. Of course you know I work at the centre – and occasionally other ones run by the council, you see. They send me wherever my services are needed.' He spoke rapidly, his words tumbling over one another.

He uncrossed his legs and crossed them the other way. 'And Blue and Ron and I are great friends. It's so sad what happened to Eddie – they told me he was missing. I'm just so relieved that someone's doing something. Now, what can I assist you ladies with? How can I help you in your investigation? I'll be ever so useful – I promise.'

Peggy's fingers paused on her keyboard. 'You think something's happened to him, then? You don't think he simply left the area?'

'Well, yes. Don't you?' Paul fingered his bow tie.

Madge bobbed her head non-committally. 'What makes you so sure of that?'

'I suppose it's obvious,' said Paul. 'Humans are social animals. Community is important to us – don't you think? Eddie had become a part of the local queer scene – at least, the *silver* queer scene, shall we say? He popped up a few years back. One day I'd never heard of him and the next he was at every party, every social event, every gathering I found myself at.'

Madge pulled a notebook from her handbag and wrote

something down. 'And you and he are close friends? Or at least, you were until he left the area?'

'Oh, yes, definitely. Sort of.' Paul cast a glance at the floor. 'Maybe not exactly. But we moved in the same circles. Obviously, as I mentioned, I attend most of Royal Tea's shows. Whenever I can, that is. And I'm also the leader and founder of the Purly Queens. I don't know if you're aware of us. We're a local knitting circle – though, naturally, we welcome people who do other types of crafting too.' He waved at Baz's embroidery as he spoke. 'We often put on shows and—'

Madge's hands stilled for a moment. 'We're aware of the Purly Queens. And we didn't invite you here to talk about them.'

Paul smoothed out the fabric of his trousers. 'I didn't know you had invited me at all. I came here to get coffee. And I should point out, I got waylaid on my way to the front counter, so I don't even have that.'

Peggy studied him. 'And I thought Clive was the leader of the Purly Queens. He certainly tells us he is often enough.'

'Clive?' Paul covered his mouth as he chuckled. 'Clive Chen? The leader?' He shook his head. 'He's only been with us for about a year! We've been going since 2013. We had a party at Deptford Does Art to celebrate our ten-year craftiversary. It was definitely me who came up with the name. That's Purly with a U, innit? And I'm the one who books us into Little Nan's Carless Car Boot sale.' He screwed up his face. 'Though now you mention it, perhaps Clive made the arrangements for last year's Christmas fair. And our booth at Deptford Pride. But I wouldn't say he's the *leader* per se.'

Peggy chuckled. 'Very interesting.'

Madge raised a hand. 'Thank you. Message received. But we're actually hoping to talk to you about Eddie.'

'Apologies – I do have a tendency to prattle.' Paul waved

dramatically as he spoke – clearly one of those people who talked with their hands. 'Eddie was such a lovely young man. I say young. Younger than us chickens, I suppose.'

Peggy clicked a few keys before looking up. 'What age is he, do you think?'

Paul pursed his lips. 'He was – oh, I don't know – maybe in his early fifties, innit? Or so. I mean, who can say, really? It's impolite to ask a lady her age and all that.'

Madge scowled. 'I thought you said Eddie was a man.'

Waving his arms, Paul grinned. 'Oh, bless. Aren't you a doll! Yes, of course, Eddie was a man. Only a figure of speech, love.'

Madge indicated Paul should continue.

'Right.' There went his hands again. They were very neat – Baz wondered if he had regular manicures. 'Let's see. What can I tell you about Eddie? He had a regular gig, cleaning a pub somewhere. He had excellent English, so that wasn't an issue. I heard he used to be a vet back in Albania. I think he did some dog-walking and pet-sitting and whatever. Anything animal related – well, anything he could get away with doing off the books, innit?'

Madge and Peggy both nodded. 'Thank you, Paul,' said Madge.

Peggy cocked her head. 'I don't suppose you have any idea where he might have gone, do you? Never heard him mention a desire to live in' – she gestured to signal she was making things up – 'Brighton or having a cousin in Sheffield. Maybe a plan to go hiking in the Peak District?'

Paul tossed his hands up. 'Sorry, ladies. I really do want to help.'

Madge's needles continued clicking away. 'What about Eddie's friends? Do you have any names you could pass on? We'd like to talk to anyone who might have any insight into where he's gone.'

He shrugged. 'Like I said, we moved in the same circles. I'll see if I can put together a list of mutual acquaintances if you think it'll help.' He turned to Baz. 'Maybe if you give me your number, I can call you if I think of something, innit?'

'Sure,' Baz heard herself say, her breath catching in her throat. *What's coming over me? What am I thinking?*

Paul smiled. 'Excellent.'

It felt like time had stopped as the others looked at her. Except it couldn't have because her heart was still thumping.

'Do you need a pen?' Madge leant over and rummaged in her carpet bag.

With a start, Baz realised they were waiting for her to write her number down. Heat rushed to her face. 'Oh, sorry. I'm sure I've got one.' With her traitorous hands quivering slightly, she hoisted her own handbag into her lap. A notepad with a small pen clipped to it occupied an outside pocket. Taking care to write legibly, she wrote her full name and mobile number on a sheet of paper, before tearing it from the pad.

Thankfully, he refrained from saying anything as he accepted it. She didn't think she could take it if he'd made a jest of the situation. It was too humiliating – she was acting the schoolgirl.

'Well.' Paul put his hands on the arms of his chair and lifted himself to his feet. 'What a lovely coincidence running into you ladies this morning. I shall have to stop by more often.' A grin spread across his face. With a little wave, he walked through the entryway to the main room – he was just short enough to avoid the need to duck.

None of the women spoke a word while Paul left – without ordering any coffee. Peggy's keys clacked, Madge's needles clicked, and Baz's needle dipped silently in and out of the fabric on her embroidery hoop.

Carole had stopped working on her project and was fixedly

staring out the window. 'Let's see how you like it,' she whispered to an urban pigeon on the other side of the glass.

The moment Paul closed the door behind himself, Peggy tutted. 'Coincidence, my arse.'

Baz felt shame burn inside her. They were investigating a man who'd gone missing – and here she was wasting time flirting! Shame on her! No wonder the girls were disgusted.

'Wasn't that interesting?' Madge studied her knitting for a moment before changing directions.

Baz opened her mouth to apologise for her unprofessional and unbecoming behaviour. But Peggy was speaking. 'The man's never been in here before and he just *happens* to discover the place while we're investigating the disappearance of one of his friends.' She shook her head. 'I don't think so.'

'Inserting himself into our investigation for no good reason.' Madge tutted. 'What do we think he wanted?'

'Do we—' Baz's voice cracked and she was forced to start the sentence over again. 'Do we not believe him? This place *is* off the main road.'

Peggy snorted.

'No,' Madge said. 'Absolutely not. He's a nosy little chancer. That's what he is.'

'Those Purly Queens are as bad as the people at the dog park.' Peggy shook her head. 'All they do is gossip.'

'Disgraceful,' Madge said. 'Now. Where were we before we were interrupted?'

Baz tried to cast her mind back to before Paul had arrived. She couldn't remember what they'd been saying.

CHAPTER 8

in which baz's skills are put to the test

BAZ SCRIBBLED over what she'd written. She tore the page from her notebook and hurled it at her computer monitor with a shriek of annoyance.

Footsteps stomped rapidly down the hall and into the flat's small study, just off the open-plan kitchen-diner-lounge. 'Are you okay?' Daisy asked, as she braced herself on the wall to pivot around the corner.

Baz let out a gruff sigh. 'Fine, fine. I just hit a dead-end is all.'

Her granddaughter leant on the desk, her blond hair falling over her face as she did so. She peered at the screen. 'Still trying to find the daycare's landlord?'

Baz reclined in her ergonomic chair. 'Looks like the whole thing is set up as a tax dodge.'

Daisy perched on the edge of the desk. 'And you'd know all about that.' She swept the hair out of her face.

Baz crossed her arms over her chest. 'Jeepers. You make it sound like I'm some sort of ... tax evader myself.' She'd almost said *criminal*, but the thought of the things she got up to with her friends made her swerve tracks at the last second.

'Only teasing.' Daisy stood back up. 'I'm sure you've come up against much worse. You'll get to the bottom of it.'

Baz felt herself deflate, like a balloon with a slow leak. 'That's the thing. I've investigated more complicated ownership structures. But I did so with the aid of expensive tools for accessing paywalled data and I had all the might of the RCMP backing me up and...' She gazed out the window.

Daisy wiggled her eyebrows. 'You all right there, Nan? Did *your* CPU crash?'

'Mmm?' Baz chewed her lower lip. 'Maybe that's what I need to do,' she muttered – more to herself than to Daisy.

Chuckling, Daisy shook her head. 'You're a million miles away right now, aren't you? How about I make us a cuppa and you tell me about this *maybe*, eh?'

Baz mentally returned to the room with a start. 'A cuppa? Listen to you! Pretty soon your friends in Canada won't recognise you!'

Daisy turned on the tap. 'Oh, don't you start. Baba said the same thing to me.'

Baz's heart stood still. 'Did he? When were you talking to him?' She knew her granddaughter was still in touch with Hari. Although there was no blood relationship between them, Baz and Hari had been together since before she was born. Daisy had lived with them for four years. To all intents and purposes, he was Daisy's grandfather. Baz shook her head. 'I'm sorry. That was rude – like you shouldn't be talking to him. I promise I didn't mean it like that. I was only curious.'

Baz swallowed as she got up and walked towards the kitchen. 'How is he?'

Daisy flicked the kettle on and then hugged her grandmother. 'No, I'm sorry, Nan. I wish I hadn't said anything.'

She released Baz's shoulders and turned to the cupboards. 'But since you asked, he's all right. He misses you too, you know.'

Annoyingly, Baz's chin began to tremble. 'Does he?'

'Just because it had to be this way doesn't mean it won't hurt.' Daisy dropped teabags into two mugs.

Baz opened her mouth to speak but no sounds came out.

Daisy reached down and squeezed Baz's shoulders. *Has the girl always been so tall?*

The kettle clicked off and Daisy went to fetch the oat milk from the fridge.

Baz caught sight of the time on the microwave. 'Oh, good heavens! I'm going to be late – and you know how Madge feels about tardiness. And I still have to go to the loo before I leave.'

Baz managed to get out of the flat swiftly. She rode like the wind to Deptford station. There were so many stations in London, it could be a bit overwhelming. Her flat was next to Deptford Bridge station – but that was different from Deptford station, which was about a ten-minute walk to the north.

When she got to the top of the ramp, the girls were visible in the distance. Baz couldn't see individual faces yet. But Peggy's mobility scooter was a dead giveaway. As she grew closer, Peggy's faded pink hair was striking. And who else but Carole would pair the bold fabric of her dress with yellow tartan rain boots? As Baz drew closer still, she could make out Madge's short curls.

Madge tapped her wrist. 'What time do you call this?'

Heat rose to her cheeks as Baz checked her own watch. But the next thing she felt was confusion. 'It's half past.'

Madge flipped her nurse's watch up and peered at it. 'And forty-three seconds. We said we'd meet at 1:30.'

Baz bit her lip. 'And I'm here? At 1:30?' She wasn't sure why her inflection was rising as though those were questions.

Peggy waved. 'Oh, give over, woman. A, she isn't late. And B, the train isn't due for another thirteen minutes.'

Drawing in a breath, Madge pulled herself up to her full height. 'That is beside the point. We set a time to meet; it's only common courtesy for everyone to be here by that time. And besides, we still have to get into the station—'

Peggy raised a liver-spotted hand and pointed. 'That station right there?' Her fingers were tipped with perpetually chipped black nail polish. She steered her scooter towards the entrance.

'—and pay for our tickets—' said Madge, hustling to keep up with Peggy.

'You mean touch our phones to the reader?' The machine bleeped as Peggy did just that.

'—and get to the platform,' Madge continued as she touched in.

The two women carried on arguing as they headed further into the station.

Baz looked at Carole and said, 'After you.' Then she felt foolish when she realised there was a second card reader next to the one both Peggy and Madge had used. 'How are you today, Carole? I feel like we never chat, just the two of us chickens.'

Carole nodded once and set off after Peggy. 'Oh, very well. Very well, indeed.' Without breaking stride, she spun around to face Baz and pointed, then continued her circuit and faced the direction she was walking in once more. 'Of course, if you have a clutch bag, it's meant to contain a basket of chicken eggs. Hardly anything remains of the ancient teachings at all. Such a shame.'

Baz frowned as they caught up with Peggy and Madge. 'I hope I didn't cause too much inconvenience with my tardiness, but I—'

'You were right on time.' Peggy crossed her arms over her

chest. 'And besides, we still have to sit out here in the frigid air for another eleven minutes waiting for the blasted train.' She pulled a pink touque from her handbag and pulled it on over her spiky hair.

'Yes, well,' Baz glanced at Madge, 'I still wouldn't want to trouble anyone. Anyways, the reason I was...' She paused to search for the right word.

'On time?' offered Peggy at the same time as Madge said 'tardy'.

Baz's breath caught. 'The reason I was *almost* late is that I got carried away researching the company that owns the building where the nursery is. I followed the trail for as long as I could. It's owned by an overseas company called Truffles Developments, which is jointly owned by a couple other companies with generic names, which are in turn owned by – I'm sure you get the idea.'

A cloud moved in front of the sun, casting the group into shadow. Madge pulled her coat's hood up. 'So did you find the answer or not?'

Before Baz could answer, the train pulled into the station. The women moved towards the area of the platform marked out for wheelchair users and others who required assistance. Apparently Peggy had notified them of their intention to take this particular train.

The attendant jumped out with the departing passengers. 'Afternoon, ladies. Off for an afternoon of shopping in Borough Market?'

Carole looked at him with a very serious look on her face. 'We're off to see the wizard.'

'Of Oz, you mean?' The attendant grabbed the portable train ramp and positioned it in front of the open train door. 'There you go, ladies.'

'Don't be ridiculous!' Carole stomped up the ramp and into the train. 'What does a werewolf have to do with anything?'

Baz smiled at the attendant as she steered her scooter up the ramp. 'Actually, we're going to drag bingo.'

'Oh, yeah?' The attendant motioned for Peggy to board next. 'Blokes dressed up as ladies, you mean? I don't hold with all that.'

Peggy drove up the same ramp. 'Maybe I don't hold with men dressed up as train attendants.'

He ran over to the edge of the platform and hung the ramp back up on the wall. Task finished, he climbed aboard the train and did ... something ... that made the doors hiss closed.

As the train pulled out of the station, the man stabbed at the button to open the door to the next carriage along.

Peggy stuck two fingers up at the man's departing back as he stepped out of sight. 'Twat.'

CHAPTER 9

in which arjun makes a surprising revelation

SEVEN MINUTES after the train pulled out of Deptford station, it arrived at London Bridge. The same attendant returned and placed the ramp again – minus the conversation.

The women exited onto St Thomas Street. Baz would've got turned around if she'd been on her own. She'd been to London Bridge a few times – on her way to Borough Market – but had always used a different exit.

They turned left, away from the Market. Carole and Peggy sped off as Baz hung back with Madge, who walked at her own pace. Madge waved at the big yellow brick building opposite the station. 'I once did a six-month secondment to Guy's.'

Baz had been to a few hospitals since moving back to London – both for matters relating to her transition and in regard to her knee. But she'd never been to Guy's. 'Oh, was it nice?'

Madge shrugged. 'A hospital is a hospital.' She chuckled as she pulled her coat tighter around herself. 'One of the anaesthetists was very handsome.'

As they passed a drab concrete block, Madge made that

noise with her tongue she often did. 'What I really didn't like was this place.'

Baz tried to look up at the nondescript office block without losing control of her scooter. 'Isn't it just offices?'

Madge scowled. 'It's the Home Office. Every morning, this street would fill up with the sad faces of asylum seekers and people with immigration issues, who were required to check in. I could see in their faces that they'd lost faith in the system. That's when I started volunteering as a host.'

The sun emerged from the clouds again as the two women turned onto a small side street. Baz was disorientated. Trusting Madge to know the way, she allowed herself to focus on the variety of architecture they passed. These streets were a warren of 1980s concrete blocks, pre-war council flats, Victorian red-brick warehouses and nurses' residences, and new-build luxury flats.

Before long, they caught up with Peggy and Carole at what appeared to be the rear entrance to a community hall. Raised voices could be heard – and not the happy kind.

As the four women walked – or rolled – around the side of the building, a park came into view. Along with a small crowd of protesters.

'Oh, lovely,' muttered Peggy. 'Those tossers are here. 'Course they bloody are.'

The lone woman in the group of protesters wore a large cardboard sign on a rope around her neck. In large red letters, it said simply: PERVERTS.

The woman spotted them and pointed a finger. 'Oi! It's them old hags from last week.' She raised her voice and bellowed, 'There's no woke cops to come to your aid this time.'

One of the men held up a handmade sign declaring: TRUST THE SIENCE. Baz shook her head.

'If you munters attack Mitch same as last time,' the man shouted, 'you should know we'll defend ourselves.'

Baz licked her lips. 'We don't want trouble.' Her voice came out a squeaky whisper and she worried she might be sick.

'That's right.' Madge positioned herself in front of Baz, blocking the angry group's view of her. 'We're just here to—'

Peggy's face tightened. 'I wouldn't mind a bit of trouble.' She took Carole's hand.

Carole smiled sweetly. 'Oh, excellent. Are we going to fight now? I'd have brought my knitting bag if I'd known.'

Mitch — Baz recognised him because of the mole beneath his ear — raised his hands. His T-shirt proclaimed the words: GAYS AGAINST GROOMERS. 'Now, now. There's no need to be so hostile. We ain't doing nuffink. Why can't we talk like the civilised adults we are?'

'I'll show you civilised,' Peggy grumbled.

Mitch raised his voice. 'They keep telling me drag is art. So how comes every drag queen I ever meet challenges me to a fight? People say dressing up like a woman is free expression. But why ain't we allowed that same freedom?' Baz fought a shiver at the murderous look in his eyes.

As his acolytes roared their approval, the front door of the community centre opened and a man stuck his head out. 'Ladies, you joining us?'

Baz felt light-headed as relief washed over her. 'Oh, thank heavens. Can we bring our scooters inside? Please?'

The burly man — wearing an arm band identifying him as a security guard — waved them in. 'Of course, of course. Welcome. Come on through.'

He let them in and then swiftly closed and barred the door. As he took up position at the peephole once again, Peggy shook her head. 'I wonder if that brute's bite is half as bad as his bark. I feel sorry for anyone who gets caught in his sights.'

Baz swallowed down her fear, though her attention was soon drawn to more pleasant thoughts as Bluebird Sofa and Shady Diana – both in full drag – were waiting just inside the door.

'Ladies, come on in,' Di said. 'Apologies for sending Errol out to rescue you, my loves. For some reason, my presence seems to inflame that crowd. I can't think why.'

The room was kitted out with three rows of tables, all facing a small stage. About half a dozen people – all of a similar age to Baz and her friends – were already seated.

Blue raised an arm – draped in a turquoise feather boa – and gestured to the tables. 'I'll tell you what, girls. Park your wheels at the back here and then come on over and mingle with the crowd. We're expecting a full house today – but it's still a while before we get started.'

Baz and Peggy put their scooters into the corner, as unobtrusively as possible in the confined space.

'Excellent,' said Blue. Today's wig was royal blue with 1940s-style pin curls. She wore a pale blue dress covered with pink and red roses. 'Now, I understand you want to mingle with the audience, chat with folks, have a bit of a natter, and see if anyone knows anything.' She took Peggy by the elbow. 'Why don't you and your lovely partner join me. I'll make some introductions.'

Di did a little curtsy, looking at Baz and Madge. 'I guess that leaves you two in my capable hands.' She extended both arms in front of herself, her fingernails long and painted a subtle rose colour that complemented her deep russet skin. Waggling her fingers, she added, 'Come on then, dolls. I promise not to bite – unless you ask nicely.'

Baz clasped Di's warm left hand. Madge did the same on Di's right. 'Lead on, then.'

Di marched them over to a table where an Asian man sat

with a White woman. Both appeared to be in their sixties. 'Madge, Baz, these wonderful folks are a couple of our regulars, Arjun and Janet.' She faced the seated pair. 'And these lovely ladies, Madge and Baz' – she indicated each woman in turn – 'are helping in the search for our missing queen.'

Di released Madge's hand and covered her mouth. 'You've heard about Sue Panova – haven't you?'

Arjun bobbled his head. 'It's a bad business. I do hope she's found safe and sound.'

Janet clutched her mug. 'Such a shame.'

Di pulled out chairs for Madge and Baz and told them to sit. 'Now, ladies. Nothing but the best for you – which is why we're offering table service today. Your choices are tea, coffee, or...' She looked up as she put a glamorous index finger to her cheek. 'Nope, that's it. Just tea or coffee. Though I suppose we could stretch to a glass of our finest tap water.' She touched her fingers to the table, fingernails clicking on the veneer surface.

'Tea for me, please, Diana,' said Madge.

Di nodded, her big blond beehive bobbing with the motion. 'Of course. And for you, my lovely?'

'I'll have a tea as well, please.' Baz ran her fingers over the laminated table top. 'Erm, I don't suppose you've got oat milk, have you?'

Fingers to her chest, Di tutted. 'Oat milk? My, my – aren't we feeling especially middle class today?' Baz felt heat begin to rise in her chest, but then Di touched her hand gently. 'I'm only throwing a bit of shade, love. Don't you worry. I'm lactose intolerant, so I've got a little carton of soya milk if that works?'

Baz exhaled. 'That would be lovely – but only if there's still enough for you. I wouldn't want you to go without on my account.'

Di waved. 'It's nothing. Back in a tick.'

As Di strutted over to a screened-off section of the community centre, Madge turned to their tablemates. 'So, Arjun and Janet, was it? You come to a lot of Royal Tea shows?'

Arjun touched his wedding band. 'I suppose we have.' He looked down at the table.

Janet put an arm around him and pulled him closer. Although the gesture was clearly born of an easy intimacy, something about it seemed platonic. 'Arjun discovered them first. My partner – Ian, he'll be here later – he and I started joining Arjun about a year back. After...' She wrapped her hand around Arjun's. 'We joined Arjun after my brother passed.'

Arjun lifted his head and smiled. 'I've known Blue since back in the day when everyone still called her Keith. Jack and I first met at one of her shows back in—' His eyes brightened as he cocked his head. 'Oh, let's see. It was after the millennium but it must have been before the big Stop the War march. I remember because Jack and I went to that together. So it must have been around 2001, 2002?'

'Hold on.' Madge pulled her notebook from her handbag. She licked her finger and flipped through pages and found what she was looking for. 'I thought they didn't start performing until 2018. That's what Di told us. I made a note of it, you see?' She tapped her notebook with her index finger.

Baz wondered what else Madge took notes of. Did she have a cabinet full of all her observations at home?

Arjun straightened his cardigan. 'Royal Tea, yes. Blue and Di started that when they decided to retire from the bar scene. But Bluebird Sofa was a south London institution for many years. She used to do all the biggest drag venues. Of course, back then drag wasn't quite so mainstream as it is now. These days, it's very hip to say you're going to a drag show. You could tell your office colleagues at the water cooler on a Monday morning and no one would bat an eye.'

He touched his finger to his lip. 'Do offices still have water coolers? I retired back in 2014. For all I know, staff gossip looks completely different these days. You still work in an office.' He nudged his sister-in-law. 'Janet works for one of the big high-street banks, you see.'

Madge was scribbling furiously in her notebook.

Janet shrugged. 'Since Covid, I only go to the office twice a week.'

Sensing the conversation was getting off track, Baz thought she should try to steer it back to Eddie's disappearance. But just then, Di returned to the table with two mugs.

'Thank you, Di.' Baz's mug was navy blue with a Cadbury's Wispa logo on the side. 'So, do you know Eddie?'

Madge's tea was served in a Charles and Diana commemorative mug from the wedding in 1981.

When Janet and Arjun looked at one another with furrowed brows, Di helped out. 'She means Sue Panova.'

Arjun touched a button on his shirtsleeve. 'Isn't it funny that another of your queens would go missing?' He looked up, raising a hand apologetically. 'Not funny-ha-ha, I mean. Funny-strange.'

Madge's eyebrows shot up as Baz's mouth fell open. 'Another?' they asked in unison.

Arjun shook his head very slightly. 'Of course! Don't you remember Fifi Galore?'

CHAPTER 10

in which a warning is served

PEGGY OPENED the front door of her building and then closed it again. Cookie reversed course ungracefully, pulling his paw back over the threshold a split second before the door closed.

'Oh heavens!' Carole clapped. 'Is John Major out there again? I've got my knitting needles – I'm ready for him. You know he's in league with the Pope. If I've told them once, I've told them a thousand times – I shan't be joining—'

'No!' Peggy snapped, causing Carole to flinch. Peggy instantly regretted her tone. 'I'm sorry, my love. It's bloody snowing – that's all. I don't trust my hips not to fail me on slippery ground. Or my ankles, for that matter.'

Carole jabbed her fists into her sides. 'We can't not go! I promised JFK I'd make cabbage rolls for the school bake sale.'

Peggy inhaled. 'I know, my love. I'm only getting my scooter. You can ride on the back if you like.' Her scooter was stored under the communal stairs, out of the way.

The caretaker had tried to tell her the space needed to be kept clear as it was the fire escape route. Which was bloody ridiculous. No one had any need to be under the stairs at any time – much less during a fire. She'd continued parking there. And he'd eventually given up on shoving notes under her door.

Snow was falling. The greenery – trees and hedges and a few patchy bits of lawn – was blanketed in white. Where the snow landed on concrete, it became a filthy brown muck. A slippery, treacherous, deadly brown muck.

Carole hopped nimbly onto the back of the scooter, and tapped Peggy on the shoulder. 'Mushy peas! Onwards to battle!'

Peggy obliged and closed her fingers around the accelerator.

Most of the time, Peggy was proud of the way she'd aged, refusing to conform to society's bizarre notions of how a woman should age – much as she'd declined to participate in the patriarchy and all its stupid gender roles. She'd done womanhood her own way all her life. And now she was doing her senior years her own way too.

But every now and then Peggy cursed her body for its failure to remain the waif she'd been for so long. Until well into her sixties, she'd been nimble and agile, strong and flexible. And now look at her. Using a mobility scooter for a walk of 100 metres. All because she was afraid of falling. She disgusted herself.

No! She refused to sink to such unworthy levels. She was using all the tools in her arsenal, same as always. That was all. If the mobility scooter made her more stable and restored her freedom, then she would use it. Because she, Margaret Persephone Trent, was growing old disgracefully and she was not ashamed of that fact.

By the time they arrived at the café, she felt strong and capable, ready to take on the world. Ready to tackle whatever nightmare was befalling these poor folks.

As Peggy parked, Baz pulled up on her own scooter – a newer, higher-end model. 'Morning, girls. Ooh, it's slippy out here today, eh?'

Peggy carefully climbed off the scooter, cane in one hand and clasping Carole's proffered hand in the other. 'And nippy. I could do without this cold.'

Baz chuckled as she swivelled in her seat, bracing herself to stand up. 'Having spent forty years living with winter temperatures of minus thirty, I think I can cope with the occasional minus one. But I'm worried I'll slip and fall on my arse.'

Carole offered Baz her free right elbow. 'Build it up with stone so strong. Dance o'er my Lady Lea.'

Baz gripped Carole's arm and the solidity of her scooter to pull herself to her feet. The three of them — well, four with Cookie — carefully made their way to the door of the café. To give him due credit, Cookie seemed to take extra care to make sure the women were okay walking on the slush-covered pavement.

Peggy acknowledged Sarah with a grunt and a wave before making her way to their table, where Madge was just taking her seat.

Ten minutes later, they were all settled and the tedious greetings and inevitable chatter about the weather had been got out of the way. Sarah had arrived with the drinks and they'd all helped themselves. It was quiet in the café, so she stayed to chat for a minute before returning to her station.

Tea in hand, Madge looked up. 'Well?'

Peggy pulled her laptop out and opened the file she'd prepared the night before. 'I did a bit of research into this Fifi Galore. That's not just her drag name, by the way — it's also her real name. She changed it by deed poll back in 2013. She's a trans woman. Her social media is an open book, so I was able to find a fair amount on her.'

Peggy tossed her espresso back and then leant forwards to return the little mug to the table. 'She's a drag performer, mostly working in and around south-east London — but she's done the odd gig elsewhere too. Not only does she perform under her own name, she's also part of an all-drag Bananarama cover band, Goddesses on the Mountain Top.'

She took a breath then continued. 'Moved from Portugal at some point in the early 2000s. No date of birth that I could find, but she looked to be around forty-five in her latest post – which stopped in May 2021. All her social media accounts just went silent. For the next year or so, it was just friends and fans, saying they hoped she was all right. Someone called Alba still replies once every few months saying she hopes Fifi's okay. Might be a sister.'

Baz looked over at Peggy. 'Both Eddie and Wilson have immigration issues – but if Fifi was here before Brexit, she should have settled status, no?'

Peggy picked up her glass of water and took a sip. Sitting back up, she wagged a finger at Baz. 'You'd think so, wouldn't you? Alas, the heartless bastards who run this country have other ideas. They never run out of ways to screw over the little folk.'

Madge frowned. 'Skip the political lecture. Just tell us what you mean.'

'It seems she returned to Portugal for seven months in 2015/2016. At the time, we were still in the EU, so it wasn't an issue.' Peggy had to bite her tongue to prevent herself from going off on another rant about the colossal act of self-harm that was Brexit. But she knew her friends didn't need to hear it. 'When she applied for settled status, they rejected her application.'

Madge's knitting needles stopped. 'Because of that trip?'

Baz's jaw fell slack. 'But she's lived here for twenty years.'

Peggy rolled her eyes. 'The system – the bloody awful system – allowed for absences of up to six months. They said people were allowed one instance of up to twelve months' absence for an "important reason".' She used her fingers to put bunny ears around the phrase. 'But, as will surprise no one, "important reasons" are left to the whims of the individual case assessor. I couldn't see what Fifi's reason was – but it got her application denied.'

Baz, who had been pouring herself a cup of tea, looked up at Peggy, aghast. 'What? But that's outrageous! Surely she could appeal?'

Peggy sniffed. 'One would assume.' She cocked her head to the side. 'Now, bear in mind, I'm only seeing her various social media accounts; we don't have access to her personal texts or emails. There's still a lot we don't know – far more than we do know, in fact.'

Madge looked at Peggy, an eyebrow raised, seemingly asking whether she was finished. Peggy nodded once.

Madge nodded back. 'What we do have in regard to ... Fifi is more than we have for Eddie or Wilson.'

Peggy looked at Madge, blinking. She made an impatient 'carry on' gesture.

Baz paused with her mug just below her lips. 'Do we? How so?'

Madge inhaled and sat up straight. 'With both Eddie and Wilson, we have no concrete evidence they're actually missing. Or rather, that they haven't simply left the area or gone into hiding. But this one is different. Fifi's disappearance was reported to the police.'

As always, Madge dropped that little bomb on her friends and then left them hanging for a minute. She bent over and pulled her notebook from her knitting bag, then sat back and proceeded to flip through the pages until she found the right one. 'I did a bit of digging too. There was a police report and an investigation under the name of—'

Peggy stabbed the air with her index finger. 'Don't you

dare.'

Madge reacted as though she'd been slapped but then carried on as though Peggy hadn't spoken. 'I know you say she changed her name by deed poll but the police report was under her previous name, which was—'

Madge didn't understand the taboo. Peggy lifted a hand and said, more softly, 'I understand, Madge. But what I'm saying is we do not speak people's deadnames. It's insensitive – it conveys the idea that you don't accept them for who they are.'

Madge's brows knitted together as tightly as the scarf she was working on. 'Even when Fifi isn't here to hear it?'

Peggy fixed Madge with a glare and then let her eyes dart left to Baz for a split second. *Come on, Madge – you're a clever woman when you want to be*, she willed her friend to understand.

Baz made a soft noise as the colour rose up from her chest and spread across her face. 'I believe what Peggy is trying to say is that referring to someone by their former name conveys to the world – or at least to everyone within earshot – that you don't believe the person when they tell you who they are. And that in turn implies to people who do hear you that maybe you don't respect *them* either. There may be circumstances in which – for practical reasons – we have to know her former name – but at this stage, I don't see that it would add anything.'

'Think of it this way, Madge,' Peggy added. 'People call you Mrs Dixon, right?'

Madge inhaled slowly, realisation dawning on her. 'Yes.'

'They don't call you by Norman's surname anymore.' Peggy looked pointedly at Madge. 'Do they?'

'They most certainly do not.' Madge sneered before composing her face. 'I understand. Thank you.' She turned to look at Baz directly. 'I'm sorry. I don't mean to give offence.'

Baz's eyes glistened as she leant over and touched Madge's hand. She might have been about to speak but the moment was interrupted by the door chime. A very tall, very large Black man entered the coffee shop.

Peggy wrinkled her nose at the man's overpowering cologne – something simultaneously fruity and woodsy and distinctly masculine. It seemed to have the opposite effect on Baz, whose nostrils were twitching and whose eyes were brightening.

In his velvety smooth baritone, he called out, 'Good morning, Sarah.' Then he ducked through the doorway – bending almost double – and stepped into the café's second room. He bent again and kissed Madge softly on the cheek.

When he stood up, he addressed the others. 'Good morning, Peggy. Good morning, Carole.' He approached Baz and held out his ham-sized hand. 'Good morning. You must be Barbara. It's lovely to meet you finally.'

'Erm, hello?' Baz's hand was entirely engulfed in his.

Madge looked up from her knitting. 'Oh, good heavens. I completely forgot you two haven't met yet. Baz, this is Chukwuma. He's an immigration lawyer. I asked him to assist Clive with his immigration application. Chukwuma, this is my friend Baz. She's a transgender woman.'

Peggy dropped her head. 'Oh, for pity's sake, Madge.'

But Baz waved her off with a small chuckle. 'It's fine.'

Chuk pulled up his trouser legs and squatted down to say hello to Cookie. And, of course, Cookie knew full well there were treats to be found in Chuk's coat pocket, so he immediately began performing his full repertoire of tricks.

When Cookie had been given the appropriate payment for his performance – and determined that no further treats were forthcoming – he retreated to his position under the table. Chuk dragged a chair over to join the women. Peggy was surprised his huge form didn't crumple the chair into nonexistence.

Sarah popped into the room with a big bowl mug. When she had set it on the table, she hugged Chuk. They chatted for a few seconds before another customer walked in the door and she left again.

Madge fixed Chuk with a stare. 'Are we expecting Clive to join us here, then?'

Chuk waved her question away. 'No, I'm meeting him in an hour. But as I had to be in the old neighbourhood, I thought I ought to pop in and see how you're getting on.' He motioned at the space around him. 'Sarah's doing brilliantly, I see.'

The beginnings of a smile tugged at Madge's lips but it was Baz who said, 'Oh, yes! This place is wonderful, isn't it? She's done a marvellous job. And it's always very busy.'

'Excellent,' he said. 'And how have you been keeping, Mags? All well, I trust?' Only Chuk got away with calling Madge 'Mags'.

'Indeed, very well. Thank you.' Her hands continued their work but she looked at him when she spoke to him. 'Cheryl's daughter has just brought my fourth great-grandbaby into the world – a little girl. Born on Christmas Day. The baby's called Layla.' She set her knitting down and retrieved her phone, then began thumbing through it, presumably in search of a photo.

Chuk put his hands together and beamed. 'How wonderful! Achebe's recently given me my own second great-grandchild.' He pulled a phone from his coat pocket – not the treat pocket, much to Cookie's disappointment – and held it up. On-screen, a baby who looked like a wizened, brown-skinned alien smiled for the camera.

In Peggy's defence, all babies looked like small, wizened aliens.

Madge finally found the image she was looking for. She proudly held the photo aloft and Peggy saw Baz do a small double-take at the image on-screen. This small, wizened alien creature had paper-white skin, a fine dusting of blond hair, and brilliant blue eyes.

Chuk took the phone from her and zoomed in on the image. 'She's just the spitting image of your Cheryl – don't you think?'

Carole, not one to miss out on the action, retrieved her phone from her handbag and proudly displayed an image of her latest grandchild – this one having moved past the shrivelled look and into the Winston Churchill stage of infant development. 'Of course, this isn't actually Harvey Junior Junior. They wanted to capture him inside the lightbox for me, but I've been very insistent that he should be allowed to develop normally. I caught the nurses trying to swap him out for a woodland fairy creature – but you can rest assured I was having none of that. And I won't let them go replacing his growth hormone neither.'

Chuk drank the last of his coffee and nodded solemnly. 'Good for you. Someone's got to look out for these precious babies.'

A look of disgust past over Carole's face and, for a moment, Peggy worried she was going to spit at Chuk. 'Don't you dare patronise me, Eugene Kaminski! I've got your number. Just because you lost your third wife to these so-called fundamentalists is no reason to try it on with me.'

Carole leant close to Peggy and grabbed her sleeve. 'I won't go down to the cellar with him. Please don't let him take me.' She shuddered and began to cry.

Peggy all but tossed her computer on the floor as she hauled herself to her feet. She took her lover in her arms and held her close. Peering over Carole's shoulder at Chuk, she whispered back, 'It's all right, my love. I've got you. Nothing's going to happen. No one's taking you anywhere – I promise.' She stroked her hair.

When Peggy felt Carole's breathing begin to slow to normal

levels, she loosened her hold. Leaning back to look Carole in the eye, she said, 'All right, that's better. You're back in the room with us now, yes?'

Carole looked up at Peggy as though just spotting her. 'Hello, Peggy! When did you get back?'

Peggy winked at her. 'Oh, I've been here a while. I'm going to take my seat now, okay?' She released Carole.

When she was back in her chair, the other four were engaged in an entirely predictable game of photo-swap with all their grandchildren and great-grandchildren. The Lord knew, Madge alone could play that game for hours on end. Peggy had lost track of how many grandkids she had – though she was fairly certain she had a total of six children.

Peggy pulled out her laptop and focused on her book. It was due to go for copy-editing just over a month from now and she wasn't quite finished with the first draft. It would take her a few more days to wrap it up. But then came the hard part – she always found the second and third draft took more out of her than the first. She flexed her fingers and began typing.

Kitty smiled. 'I might use that in my next play.'

Will opened his mouth wide. 'You wouldn't. I'm using it in *my* next play. I already told you that.'

Kitty batted those long eyelashes that Will never could resist. 'Then you'd better get writing. If I get to it first, it's mine.' He leant in close and touched Will lightly on the nose.

Peggy was so absorbed in her work that two people had walked into their sanctum and approached the group before she even noticed them.

'Morning, Granny,' said Peter as he ducked into the room. Something about the look on his face made Peggy suspect this wasn't a social call. But then he spied Chuk and a broad grin brightened his face. 'Grandad! I hadn't expected to find you here. Is everything okay?'

Baz showed a flicker of surprise at that. But only a flicker. When it came to other people's lives, she was pretty much unflappable. Peggy wished she showed herself as much grace.

The big man stood up and embraced his grandson. 'Peter! I didn't expect to see you either. I'm in the area on business, so I stopped in for a chat. I suppose you're living the police officer's dream, eh? Patrolling every coffee shop in the area?'

Peter grimaced at his grandfather but didn't reply. His new partner was a young woman with a round face and tufts of blond hair sticking out from under her uniform hat. She stood in the corner of the room with her hands tucked under her stab vest, looking awkward as all get out.

Chuk took Peter by the elbow and steered him into the café's main room. 'Come on, son. Only teasing. Let me buy you a coffee and we can chat before I have to dash to my appointment.'

'I'm here on official business actually.' Poor Peter – he actually tried to stop walking.

'Nonsense,' said Chuk in that velvety smooth bass voice of his. If he ever gave up on the law, Peggy would hire him to narrate her audiobooks. Peter was whisked along into the main room.

Peter's partner darted her eyes to the women then back towards the door. 'Erm,' she said, biting her lip. 'I'll just...' She made to take a step forwards, then seemed to change her mind. Eventually, she took up position, standing in the metre-thick doorway between the café's two rooms. She was short enough to stand upright.

Peggy bit her tongue to keep from chuckling.

Baz spun around in her seat and squinted at the officer's name badge. 'Constable Turner, is it?'

PC Turner's eyes darted towards the front door and then back towards Baz. She relaxed a smidge – but only a smidge. 'Yes.' She smiled tentatively. 'Keeley.'

Baz shook Keeley's hand. 'I'm Baz. It's lovely to meet you. You're Peter's new partner, I take it?'

The young officer smiled more genuinely this time. 'That's right. I completed the gateway programme a few months ago. After... Well, Peter needed a new partner, so he's been showing me the ropes.'

'I'm sure he's a very good teacher,' Baz said.

The girl nodded. 'He really is.'

Chuk appeared on the other side of the doorway. He bent at the waist and smiled at the women. 'It was lovely seeing you all.'

Peggy raised a hand in farewell.

When Chuk moved out of the way, Peter ducked through the door. He gave PC Turner one of the two coffee cups he was carrying and approached the women. Then, with his free hand, he removed his hat. 'Good morning, ladies.' He looked at his feet.

'Go on, young Peter.' Madge studied him curiously. 'Whatever it is you've come here to say, spit it out.'

He pursed his lips. 'Right. The thing is...'

Peggy groaned internally. This was going to take all morning.

'I've been asked to come and tell you not to—'

Madge leant away from him and glared at him over her glasses. 'You're going to tell Granny what she can and cannot do – is that it?'

Peggy snuck a glance at Keeley, who was biting down on her lip for all she was worth.

Peter shuffled from foot to foot. When he spoke, his voice was firmer. 'I've been instructed to ask you — all of you — politely — to stop investigating.'

Madge folded her arms over her chest. 'Why should we?'

Peter ran a hand over his tight curls. 'Surely you can see this is police business. They've... That is, we've already run a task force looking into the missing men.' The pitch of his voice was higher than normal — almost pleading.

Three women spoke at the same time in a cacophony of voices.

Rubbing the back of his neck, Peter said, 'One at a time. Please.' He pointed at Madge. 'Granny, what was your question?'

Madge frowned. 'Can't have been a very effective task force if they're all still missing — can it?'

Peter took a deep breath and turned to Baz. 'Ms Spencer, what was it you said?'

Baz swallowed. 'Sorry, I said it's missing *people*, not missing *men*. Fifi Galore was a woman.'

Peter nodded. 'I'm sorry. I didn't realise. Okay.' He turned to Peggy. 'Ms Trent, your turn.'

Before responding, Peggy studied his face for a moment. 'This task force... When was it?'

'Operation Wellesley ran from December 2020 to August 2021. And...' Peter raised a hand in a stop gesture. 'And it found no evidence of any foul play in any of the cases.'

Peggy scoffed. 'No evidence.' She shook her head in disgust.

Baz tugged on her ear and looked out the window for a moment. 'So, Fifi wasn't the first? I mean, they wouldn't have formed a task force to investigate disappearances unless there was more than one. Do you even know about Wilson or Eddie?'

'Who?' Peter asked, then raised a hand, palm facing outwards. 'No, never mind. If you have reports of people who've gone missing, you need to make an official report to the police.' He emphasised the final words with nods. 'Just ... please, ladies. My sergeant asked me to have a word with you – off the record. If you don't let matters rest, they'll charge you with obstructing a police officer under section 89.2 of the Police Act 1996.'

He took a drink of his coffee. 'Now, no one wants to see you charged – least of all me. So please, drop it. Okay?' No one said anything. After a moment, he mumbled, 'Sorry,' then turned to the exit. 'C'mon, Keeley. Bye, Granny. Bye, Aunties.'

Peggy could barely contain a chuckle until the door closed behind the pair. Before long, all four women were doubled over and howling with laughter.

CHAPTER 11

wherein someone is not who he appears be

BAZ FLUNG the café door open with far more force than she'd intended to. It bounced off the wall with a clatter, startling her and making her squeak. It didn't help matters that the interior of the shop was so dark compared with the bright sun outside. She couldn't even see if she'd inconvenienced anyone. 'I'm sorry, I'm sorry sorry so.' She was in such a rush that she tripped over her words and they tumbled out in the wrong order.

Madge's voice sounded from the doorway to the second room. 'Baz? What on earth has got into you? I'm all for civility – but you just apologised to a pot plant.'

Heat flushed Baz's cheeks. Her eyes were adapting to the relative darkness – which wasn't dark at all – of the café and she could see the object of her floundered apology.

'Come on.' Madge held out her arm for Baz to take. 'Let's get settled. You can order your tea once the rush dies down.'

On the far side of the room, a cluster of people stood at the bar waiting to order or pay or receive their drinks. Baz waved an apology at them before following Madge into the second room.

Once the pair were seated in their customary spots, Madge fished out her knitting. 'Now. Are you going to tell me what's brought you here so early?'

'Am I early?' Baz pulled her embroidery from her bag and heaped it onto her lap. Then she grabbed a stack of papers she'd printed out and piled them atop.

Madge cocked her head. 'Our arrangement has always been to meet after nine o'clock once the commuter rush dies down. It is currently' – Madge checked the nurse's upside-down watch-badge she always wore – '08:47 am. So I repeat my question. What brings you here so early?'

Baz smoothed her papers. 'I should probably wait for Peggy and Carole.'

A few people had exited the café since she'd arrived. 'Actually, I should go and order.' She lifted the various items off her lap and then held them in the air above herself. 'Oh, good grief. I'm not sure why I've got this stuff out so soon.' She set the items down on Carole's chair before pulling herself to her feet. Then she wasted several seconds packing the items back into her bag. All the while she could feel Madge's eyes on her. 'Won't be a moment. Do you need anything from the ... from the other room?'

Madge shook her head, so Baz headed to the counter, passing Peggy and Carole, who were just arriving.

Baz waited as the customer ahead of her in the queue placed his order. Olena, Sarah's employee, was working at the cash register.

Are they still called cash registers now that no one uses cash?

Olena smiled and tilted her head. 'Morning, Baz. Everything all right? You seem a bit ... what's the word? Foostered – is that it?'

Baz chuckled. 'Flustered? Yes, I suppose I am that.'

When she finished placing her order, she went back to join her friends. Fizzing with excitement, she dropped into her chair. She arranged herself and pulled her craft bag onto her lap, then looked up to find three faces eagerly watching her. The three faces, of course, belonged to Peggy, Madge, and Cookie. Carole was studying a dead wasp on the windowsill.

Baz gave Cookie a quick pat as she faced her friends. 'You girls are never going to believe what I uncovered. Never in a million years.'

Peggy arched an eyebrow. 'We certainly won't if you don't spit it out.'

'Come on,' said Madge. 'Fill us in on what's got you all in a tizzy this morning. I assume you've made progress on the missing persons case.'

Baz was in the middle of bending to retrieve her papers from her bag. She sat back up again. 'The missing persons case? But the police told us to drop that.'

Madge stared over her glasses. 'Despite what my grandson may think, I'm not in the habit of taking orders from children.'

Baz removed her papers from the craft bag and smoothed them again. 'Well, no. Of course not. But he's...' She blinked and shook her head. 'Erm, it isn't about that at all, actually. You see...'

Just then, a figure emerged in the doorway, and Baz's stomach fluttered.

'Halloo, my lovelies,' said Paul. 'Isn't it a fine sunny day in London? How are we all doing?'

A second figure emerged from behind him. 'Wagwan, ladies?'

Peggy gave a melodramatic sigh that probably shook the earth in the neighbouring boroughs. 'I see Clive is instructing you in the art of picking the worst moment to interrupt people's conversations.'

'Clive,' Madge growled. And then, more cordially, she added, 'Good morning, Paul.'

Baz wasn't sure whether what she was feeling would be classed as light-hearted or light-headed – perhaps a mix of both. 'Paul, what a surprise! It's lovely to see you again.' She swallowed. 'And you too, Clive.' Though she didn't really mean that last part.

Paul waved expressively. 'I ran into Clive this morning at that new Sainsbury's on the high street. Isn't it incredible! We've now got a Tesco, an Asda, and a Sainsbury's on our little high street. Imagine that! Anyhow, we got to chatting and we thought we'd pop in and see how you're getting on with your investigation.'

At some point in his little monologue, he'd rested his hand lightly on Baz's arm. Where his skin touched hers, she glowed with heat.

When Paul caught her looking at his hand, he removed it swiftly. 'All right. Go on – spill it,' he prodded. 'What's the buzz? What's the scoop? What have you learnt? Don't keep us in the dark.'

Peggy removed her fingers from her keyboard and crossed her arms over her chest. 'What we have learnt is that the police don't take kindly to little old ladies who investigate crimes.'

Both Paul and Clive gasped. 'What?'

Madge kissed her teeth. 'Someone didn't like us digging our noses into their business.'

Baz felt her heart rate spike. 'You think someone—' She lowered her voice to a whisper. 'You think someone told the police we were ... investigating?'

Madge's knitting needles clicked away. 'I think that's exactly what happened.'

Peggy nodded. 'We're four harmless old women. What do the police care if we're looking into a cold case? It's not as if they're doing anything. So far as we can tell, they're not even aware of the latest two victims.'

'Now, hold on,' said Madge at the same time as Clive asked, 'Latest two? What do you mean, *latest* two?'

Clive looked at Madge, holding up his hands in the style of someone surrendering. 'Ladies first – I insist.'

Madge glowered at Peggy. 'We haven't reached the conclusion there are *any* victims. We have heard tell of three m...' She paused. 'I'm sorry, that was a mistake. We've heard tell of three people who ... are missing.'

Peggy shrugged. 'What? I said the latest two – which implies the existence of a total figure greater than two. And, given we're aware of three missing people, my statement was accurate.'

'The word you used was victims.' Madge crossed her arms over her chest.

Peggy's eyes moved from side to side and then back to Madge. 'Yes, we're aware of three victims. That is a statement of fact.'

Madge's hands stilled, as did the needles they held. 'No, that is a conclusion. You pride yourself on your deep understanding of words and their meanings. I don't see how the distinction can be lost on you.'

Baz didn't like the two women arguing. Part of her almost wanted to step in and try to broker peace. But she'd learnt early on in their friendship that both Peggy and Madge seemed to enjoy their conflicts. Her attempts to assuage matters had ended in one of two ways. Either the women ignored her and carried on bickering ... or the far worse option: they joined forces in turning their barbed words on Baz.

'The immigration system in this country is designed to keep

people out,' Peggy said firmly. 'Our government victimises and villainises immigrants. They put the blame for their own misdeeds on the very people targeted by those misdeeds. People like *you*, Madge.'

The emphasis Peggy put on that one word reminded Baz that of everyone in their group, it was Madge who was the immigrant.

Baz, of course, had been an immigrant for much of her life – but now she'd returned to the country of her birth – of her formative years. She was the one who *felt* like an outsider. She was the one with the strange, unplaceable accent. Of the four of them, Baz was the one who sometimes looked the wrong way before crossing the street or used words like *eavestrough* or *touque* or *hydro* or the face-reddening, unforgivable *homo milk*.

But Madge... Madge had lived in the UK since she was a toddler. In fact, she'd lived in this very neighbourhood longer than any of the rest of them. Madge had come to London in the 1950s. She'd been in Deptford ever since. She'd grown up here, studied here, worked here. According to Madge, she'd been married three and a half times – whatever that meant – here.

Peggy was still talking. 'So, yes, Madge. I chose my words deliberately. You may choose to believe those individuals vacated the area of their own volition. That's fine. I disagree – I think the evidence is beginning to paint a clear picture of them coming to some sort of harm. But that is beside the point. Every single one of them is a victim of our government's cruel immigration policies. You won't convince me otherwise.'

Madge snorted. 'Yes, all right. You've got me there. We're in agreement on that much. But I still maintain there's no evidence that any of the individuals in question – Eddie,

Wilson, or Fifi – did anything other than leave the area under their own volition.'

'Fifi?' Paul was in the middle of dragging a couple of chairs over from another table. 'Hang on, Fifi Galore? I always wondered what happened to her. She used to be a regular at Duckie. Of course, this was back in the day when it used to be at the Vauxhall Tavern – before it moved to the Eagle.'

Paul dropped himself into one of the chairs he'd procured – closer to Baz than the one he offered Clive. He nudged the other man in the shoulder. 'We met at Duckie. Do you remember?'

Clive leant away as he pivoted to look at his friend. 'What on earth are you talking about?'

Paul sat up stiffly and tugged on his earlobe. 'What do you mean – what am I talking about? You and I – the drag show? Goddesses were performing. Remember that all-drag cover band? They were doing "Cruel Summer", which really was cruel because, as I recall, it was a particularly blustery March at the time. Anyhoo, in the middle of the song—'

Clive blinked. 'I remember it well, but clearly you don't.'

Paul waved. 'Go on then. Enlighten me. What am I forgetting?'

'That's not where we *met*.' Clive shook his head. 'We met at the George and Dragon in Blackheath. The Duchess was on stage and you' – Clive stabbed a finger at Paul – 'tripped over that ridiculous feather boa and you spilt your drink on me and—'

Throwing his hands in the air, Paul exclaimed, 'That was a year after the Bananarama incident.'

Madge coughed impatiently.

Baz was amused by the good-natured bickering the men were doing, which was probably quite hypocritical of her. She'd only just been thinking about how uncomfortable she was when Peggy and Madge did the same thing. Perhaps it was because she was an outside observer with Paul and Clive – like she was watching the exchange on television. Or maybe it was something about the nature of the argument.

Peggy drummed her fingers on the arms of her chair. 'Gentlemen.'

Paul and Clive continued bickering.

Peggy pulled her cane from behind her chair and stretched it out over the table, jabbing Clive's knee with the rubber ferrule.

'Ow!' Clive slapped the cane away. 'What'd you do that for?'

Madge fixed Clive with a glare. 'We have important business to attend to. And you two are behaving like a pair of children.' She made a flicking motion. 'Now go on, off you pop. We'll let you know when we have more information for you.'

Clive jabbed his thumb in Paul's direction. 'He started it.' Nevertheless, he stood up to leave.

Madge made a show of setting her knitting project down and crossing her arms over her breasts. Her eyes were fixed on Clive. 'Get out.'

Clive grabbed Paul's arm and tugged him to his chair. 'Please. I promise we'll behave. Only we're worried. Eddie's been missing for two weeks. And now you're saying there are other missing men.'

'People.' Baz winced. She hadn't meant to say that.

Paul turned and studied her, his head tilted to the side in that way her dog used to do. 'What?'

She wasn't sure she should say anything but he sat there, looking at her, waiting for her to speak. 'People. Clive said missing men. But Fifi's a woman – a trans woman. So, in fact, it's missing people, you see. Not just men.'

Paul touched her knee – just for a second. 'Was she? I'm

sorry – I hadn't realised.' He looked at the others. 'You've made progress, then?'

Peggy scoffed. 'Some. Not much. We've discovered three missing people – all queer. Two gay men and a trans woman. All with immigration ... challenges. But the disappearances are spread out over a period of several years. It might be nothing.'

'Doesn't sound like nothing to me.' Paul took a deep breath. 'What's your next move?'

'We were trying to discuss that,' Madge said pointedly, 'when the pair of you showed up and interrupted.'

Paul got to his feet. 'Promise me you'll call us when you know more – will you?'

He looked Baz in the eye and she could feel heat prick her skin. 'I will.'

'Fine. You win – we're leaving.' Clive stood up too. 'But please keep digging.'

Once the men were gone, Peggy closed her computer. 'Finally.'

Madge poured herself another cup of bright red tea from her thermal carafe. 'All right, go on then, Baz. Spill it.'

Baz's heart raced and her throat seemed to close up. 'What? He's just a friend!'

Peggy scrunched up her nose. 'What in heaven's name are you talking about?'

Madge took a long drink of her tea then set the cup down and picked her knitting back up and studied it. 'Before that pair of idiots came in and got us all distracted, you were about to tell us something important. So go on.'

The vice that held Baz released; she could breathe again. She almost laughed. 'Oh, yes. Sorry, sorry.' She looked down at her lap and realised the papers she'd tried so hard to keep crease-free had been in her grip the entire time. The entire stack was rumpled beyond salvaging. 'Oh.'

The other women watched her as she smoothed the papers out as much as she could. She swallowed. 'Remember I told you about the shell corporation?'

Both Peggy and Madge looked at her, not comprehending.

Baz took a deep breath. 'You recall I started looking into the building where the day nursery is located, right? I followed the trail for a while but it was owned by an off-shore company – tax avoidance thing. I dug and dug but without the tools I had when I was still working – well, I didn't get very far.'

Madge bent over the table and picked up Baz's teapot and motioned to her cup. Baz nodded and Madge poured her some then added oat milk.

Baz accepted the cup gratefully and took a drink. She allowed the brew to infuse her with the calm determination she needed. After a moment, she continued. 'So, in the end I called in a favour from an old colleague. She called me back yesterday afternoon.'

Peggy made a rolling gesture with her left hand.

Baz smoothed the papers again. 'I managed to get the name of the person at the heart of all this.'

'Who is it?' Madge frowned.

Baz studied the papers again, though by this time, she had memorised the name. 'He's called Crispin Caspian Todd-Mitchell. CCTM. Those initials appear in several of the shell company names.'

Peggy rubbed her face. 'Mr Four First Names sounds a right twat. But I don't see how that helps us.'

'Crispin Caspian Todd-*Mitchell*,' Baz repeated. She leafed through the papers in front of her until she found the right one. 'I spent about an hour researching him last night. There's very little info on him. Plenty on the family – but not much on Crispin. But early this morning I made a bit of a breakthrough.

Do you recognise him?' She handed the paper, with its greyscale image of the man in question, to Madge.

Madge pushed her glasses up her nose and held the paper close, studying it. 'He doesn't look familiar to me.'

Peggy took the page from Madge and held it at arm's length, squinting. 'I don't recognise him.' She shook her head. Touching Carole on the knee, she added, 'What about you, love? Do you know this man?'

Carole chuckled. 'If it isn't Mr Gays Against Groomers. It's a shame I'm doing crochet today.'

'What?' Peggy scrunched up her face.

Baz bit her lip. She knew exactly what Carole meant.

Carole looked Peggy in the eye. 'I did tell him I could take him. Mind you, you were the one to knock him down that first time.'

Peggy looked at Carole and then at the paper. 'The thug leading the anti-drag protests?'

'Give me that.' Madge snatched the paper from Peggy and brought it almost to her nose. 'This Crispy Crunchy Todmorden is the scoundrel who's accosted us at the shows?'

Baz leant back in her chair and smiled. She'd surprised both Peggy and Madge – that was something to be proud of.

CHAPTER 12

in which things are worse than previously suspected

PEGGY DIDN'T SURPRISE EASILY. She liked to think she could spot a toff a mile away. After all, she'd grown up with them. And, however much she denied it, in some ways she was still one of them. Sure, she'd walked away from her background – turning her back on her family's wealth and privilege. She'd made her own way in the world and hadn't accepted money from anyone in her family in more than fifty years.

But a person's upbringing never left them. Not really.

So what did this Mitch person see when he looked at Peggy? Did he see the crusty old punk most people did? Or did he see Margaret Persephone Trent, daughter of Edward 'Stucky' Trent of Trent Pharmaceuticals and the Conservative peer Maude Wolston Trent, better known as Baroness Bromley?

Perhaps he could see the Peggy Trent who spent her formative years in a home with a name rather than a number. Orchard House had been featured in Ernest Newton's *Book of Houses*, published in 1890. Or the Peggy who'd spent seven years at Wycombe Abbey, a prestigious boarding school for girls.

If Peggy hadn't seen past Mitch the thug to Crispy Crunchy Todmorden, as Madge had dubbed him, then maybe he hadn't seen beyond Peggy the pink-haired lesbian. Who could say?

When Peggy looked up, Baz tapped the papers still in her lap with a ruby fingernail. Unlike Peggy's fingernails, Baz's polish was never chipped. 'I've got a long list of shell companies he's got an interest in. Through them, he owns properties all over the UK, including quite a few in this neighbourhood.'

'Well, well, well,' Peggy muttered.

Baz took another drink of her tea before setting the mug down. 'He owns commercial buildings, flats, houses, hotels, pubs – from ex-council flats to grand country estates and everything in between. Not only does he own the nursery premises, he also owns the flat upstairs from you. Where Emmy and Amrita live. Where Wilson lived until he went missing.'

'Rich landlord owns multiple properties.' Peggy shrugged. 'This isn't news. It's *interesting* – but I don't see what use it is to us.'

Baz dropped her voice to a harsh whisper. 'No, I suppose it's not news. But what he's doing is *illegal*. If HMRC got wind of his activities, he'd end up owing the tax man. Maybe even a custodial sentence. I don't have enough information to hazard a guess at how much he's earning from this property empire, but we're definitely talking about significant figures.'

Madge relinquished one of her knitting needles and stroked her chin. 'Hmm. So the same scoundrel harassing the lovely folks from Royal Tea – performers and audience members alike – is also responsible for trying to put innocent, hard-working Debs out of business?'

'Indeed.' Peggy tapped her index finger on the arm of her chair. 'I propose we set the info you discovered on this despicable fat cat aside for a while as we consider the missing persons case.'

Madge was already back to her knitting. 'I concur.'

Baz's shoulders fell. 'Oh.'

Peggy lifted both hands and held them up, palms outwards. 'No one is suggesting we not act on the information you've obtained. We absolutely should. We're merely proposing to give this some time to percolate while we discuss the other case.'

Baz brightened again. 'Ah, okay. Thank you.'

Peggy opened her computer once more and glanced at the words on-screen.

> Kit sighed. 'Do you really have to go so soon?'
>
> Will pulled himself from his lover's arms. 'We both know I can't get caught here.' He held up the stump of his candle. 'This is barely enough to get me home as it is. If I don't go now, I'll get caught here – and then where would we be?'

Then she closed her writing project and opened the new file she'd created last night, MisPer. It brought together their findings so far. Scrivener could be useful for more than just books. 'After we left yesterday and based on what the police—'

Carole shook her head and began a foul-mouthed rant.

However much Peggy wanted to speak, it was never wise to interrupt Carole. Fortunately, it wasn't a particularly long rant. When Carole finished providing her thoughts on the Metropolitan Police, Peggy continued. 'Based on what they told us about Operation Wellesley, I did a bit of digging.'

Madge nodded. 'Very good.'

Peggy ran her finger around the laptop's trackpad, not clicking anything. 'One thing I noted in Peter's little ... speech was that Fifi went missing while the task force was active, which implies that there were enough people reported missing even before her to raise suspicions.'

When the others indicated their agreement, Peggy carried on. 'There wasn't much about Operation Wellesley online – just a few short articles and blog posts. That gave me the names of three more vic—' She held a hand up to Madge, forestalling any further arguments about what led to the disappearances. 'Three more people who seem to fit the pattern. The disappearance of Hassan Abbas was reported in 2018. The next was Samuel Musa in 2019. And Moses Okello in late 2020.'

Baz frowned. 'Is there anything that connects them to Eddie, Wilson, or Fifi?'

'Well.' Peggy took a breath. 'Excellent question. I wondered the same thing myself.' She ran her finger over the screen, trying to find her place. 'Now, it was Moses Okello's disappearance that spurred the task force. The police were swift to connect it to the Samuel Musa case. Okello was reported missing by his estranged partner, Floyd Gallo.'

'So he's gay.' Madge nodded. 'That's a link.'

Peggy tried not to chuckle. 'We can't say for certain what his orientation is. But presumably he's not straight. The police report showed that he and Floyd Gallo were in a relationship from 2019 until the summer of 2020.'

'What about the immigration angle?' Baz was rubbing her chin.

Peggy waggled an index finger at Baz. 'Aha. Now that is the question. I couldn't find anything for certain – at least not that was available publicly. So I did the same as you.'

Baz cocked her head. 'How do you mean?'

'I reached out to a former colleague to see if they could dig up any more details,' Peggy said.

Baz opened her mouth but then closed it.

Something dawned on Peggy – Baz didn't know about her career. 'I was a journalist. Mainly I covered politics – but I did make a few forays into police corruption and the like. Most of my former colleagues are now retired but I do still have a few contacts. I emailed a couple people who I thought might be able to assist in getting to the heart of this. The *Independent* ran a story on Operation Wellesley back in early 2021. The reporter wasn't anyone I knew, but I called a former colleague to see if she could dig up a bit of dirt for me.'

'And?' Madge was squinting at the scarf she was knitting. She plucked a strange little tool from her case and did something to the wool.

'And she replied overnight.' Peggy had been pleased when she'd seen just how much information her young friend had turned up – until she realised she'd have to spend an evening socialising with her and her insufferable husband to make up for it.

Peggy sighed. 'The paper did a freedom of information request to get everything the police had. She sent the file over. Some of it was redacted of course, but I read through what they had.' She scrolled down to the appropriate spot in her notes. 'Hassan, Samuel, and Moses were all caught in our immigration system, fitting the pattern we've observed so far. However, the police don't seem to have picked up on whether they were part of the LGBTQIA+ community. But their countries of origin are ... well, they're not exactly known for their wholehearted embrace of queer people.'

Baz opened her bag and retrieved her embroidery work. She pulled the needle towards herself, a long steely blue thread trailing. 'What countries are those?'

'Pakistan, Nigeria, and Uganda – respectively. We know Moses had a long-term boyfriend but we don't know anything about Hassan or Samuel. It's entirely possible they weren't part of the community. But...' Peggy picked a piece of lint from her jeans. 'Hassan's friends were interviewed and a few of them mentioned pubs they'd visited together. Lo and behold, they all run occasional drag nights. We don't know whether he'd been there for that, of course, but it's a bit of an interesting titbit, I thought.'

'Excellent,' said Madge. 'I had a word with young Peter last night.'

Peggy bit down on a chuckle. 'I'll bet you did.' She wished she could've been a fly on the wall for that conversation. Then again, Peter was a decent sort. Madge would have given him a dressing down he wouldn't soon forget.

'I managed to get him to fill me in on some of the details of this Operation Wellesley,' said Madge.

Baz's jaw fell slack. 'You did? Good heavens.'

Madge had a certain gleam in her eye. 'Of course I did.'

Baz narrowed her eyes. 'How on earth did you manage that?'

'Well.' Madge touched her hair. 'He agreed to fill me in on a few little details to satisfy my own curiosity.'

'And why would he agree to do that?' asked Peggy.

Madge released her needles again. 'He may have done so on the condition we desist our investigation. Since the matter had drawn to a conclusion and the police found no evidence of foul play, he says we have every reason to drop the matter.'

The women sat in the relative silence of the busy urban café for a few seconds.

And then, one by one, all four women burst into fits of hysterical laughter. Every time she thought she'd got control of herself, Peggy would look up and catch the eye of one of her friends.

Sarah flew around the corner into their little room. She glanced around the group and thumped herself on the chest. 'What on earth is going on in here? I thought someone was being murdered!'

Peggy looked down at her lap, blinking rapidly and waving a hand in front of her face. She used her sleeves to wipe the tears from her eyes. 'Sorry, Sarah. I regret to inform you we are all very much alive.'

Baz held two fingers to her lips and shook her head.

Madge pulled a tissue from one of her pockets and dabbed at her eyes. 'Sorry, dear. Didn't mean to scare you.'

Carole looked up at Sarah. 'I told them. I did. But the joke's on them.' She beckoned Sarah to come close. When she did, Carole whispered, 'I don't even like clam chowder.' She burst into giggles again.

'Okay.' Sarah stood upright and backed away. 'You're sure you're all okay, yes?'

Peggy, Baz, and Madge all nodded.

Sarah put a hand on her hip. 'Okay, but don't go scaring me like that again.' Before heading back to the main room, she cleared the dirty dishes off the other tables.

The women stayed quiet for a few minutes, as they fought to regain their composure. Or at least, it was a battle for Peggy. She could feel the urge to cackle bubbling up from deep inside her.

At length, Madge cleared her throat. 'Anyhoo. Much of what young Peter told me aligned with what you said.'

Madge used her knitting to gesture at Peggy. 'The police don't seem to have connected the dots with regard to the sexual orientation of the missing people. But they did pick up on the immigration angle. Hassan and Samuel both came to this country as students. I'm not sure how Moses first arrived in the UK. Two of them applied for asylum, whereas Hassan had actually applied for a work visa after he finished his studies. All three had their applications denied. I don't know the reasons behind the rejections. But they were all classed as over-stayers.'

Madge paused to study her knitting for a moment. She undid a few stitches before starting back up again. 'Now, what your journalist friend was missing was that the police looked at another disappearance in connection with Operation Wellesley. They decided they didn't have enough to act on that case. I got the name of that individual as well.' She set her knitting down and pulled out her notebook. 'Abdullah Sultana.'

Peggy pressed her forehead. 'So, we're talking seven missing people. People who've just – poof – vanished from our community. People do not disappear.' She thumped her fist onto the arm of her chair, startling Cookie.

'Peggy—' Madge began.

Peggy wagged an angry finger at her friend. 'Don't start with me. Don't you dare. One person up and leaves his home, well, maybe he had good reason. Two people?' She bobbled her head. 'Maybe. But we're talking about seven people who've disappeared. Seven! I'm sorry but no. This is not a coincidence.'

'Peggy—' Madge tried again.

Peggy's muscles clenched and twitched. 'I don't want to hear it, Madge. You can't possibly believe that seven people can just disappear and we—'

She looked down at Madge's hand on her arm.

'Peggy,' Madge said softly. 'I believe you.'

Peggy crossed her arms over her chest. 'Go on.'

Madge sighed. 'After speaking to Peter, I rang Chukwuma. We had a good long chat. Samuel was one of his clients. And this other man the police mentioned, Abdullah, was a client of one of his lawyer friends. They've been convinced for a while that there's something going on. Samuel's case for asylum was solid. They were weeks away from getting a decision.'

Peggy wanted to shake her head. Of course it would take Chuk's intervention to persuade Madge. Still, she'd take it.

CHAPTER 13

wherein madge gets flustered

BAZ PUSHED the plate away from herself and exhaled. 'I couldn't eat another bite.'

Peggy, who had dyed her hair electric blue overnight, got a cheeky look in her eye as she leant closer to Daisy. 'You know, when Baz invited us for lunch today, we all balked.'

'Oh, yeah?' Daisy gave her a small smile. 'Why's that, then?'

Baz looked down and brushed a crumb from her placemat. Cookie was on it in an instant. 'For a moment, I assumed you objected to eating vegan food. But then I realised I'd neglected to mention the most important detail.'

Daisy's smile became a chuckle. 'Would that be the fact I'd be the one cooking, by any chance?'

Peggy tapped her nose twice. 'Indeed. I prefer my lunch to be of the edible sort.' She turned to Baz. 'Though I will say this traybake is delicious. What did you call it? Namayo?'

'Thank you.' Baz sat up taller and gave a small nod. 'It's a Nanaimo bar.'

Peggy took another bite and savoured it for a moment. 'The flavours are different, but it's similar to an Italian cremino.'

Madge flipped up the nurse's watch pinned to her chest. 'We'd best get a move on if we want to be on time.' She pushed her chair back from Baz's dining table and stood.

As Madge began collecting everyone's dishes, the others got up.

Daisy tried to take the stack of plates from Madge. 'I can do that. Honestly.'

Madge made a tiny shake of her head. 'Don't be ridiculous. Won't take us more than a few minutes to get this all washed up.'

Daisy raised her hands in surrender. 'Okay, okay. You can stack them over there next to the dishwasher. I draw the line at washing the dishes. How about that, eh?'

Madge arched an eyebrow and studied the much-taller woman for a few tense seconds. 'As I said, we'll get everything loaded into the dishwasher before we go.'

———

THE OLDER WOMEN bundled up in their coats and hats and sturdy shoes.

'Thank you for the lovely lunch,' said Madge.

'You behave yourself, young man.' Peggy bent to give Cookie a quick cuddle before standing upright and addressing Daisy. 'And thank you for looking after this big lump for a few hours.' The giant dog wasn't brave enough to be left home alone.

Daisy looked up from where she was sitting on the floor, playing some sort of game with the dog. 'You're kidding, right? I'd happily pay *you* for the privilege of hanging out with him. I've got our whole afternoon planned out. First up is a trip to Hilly Fields. Then I've got some games to sharpen his brain.'

Peggy snort-laughed. 'Good luck with that. I love him dearly, but there's nothing there to sharpen.'

Daisy covered Cookie's ears with her hands. 'Don't you listen to her. She's just being mean.'

Madge looked pointedly at Daisy. '*She* is the cat's mother.'

Baz tried not to let a chuckle escape her lips. There had to be some kind of law somewhere that dictated if anyone ever referred to someone as 'she' when the 'she' in question was present, an uptight older woman would pop her head up like a grammar jack-in-the-box and declare that '*she* is the cat's mother'.

What does that even mean?

Peggy rolled her eyes. 'Haven't you been paying attention, Madge? Surely, if anything, *she* is the dog's mother.'

Several minutes later, the four women set out from the front door of Baz's tower block – two on their scooters and two walking.

As she steered along the pavement, Baz tried hard not to think of the time they'd all set out from her place to have a very awkward and ill-advised meeting.

When they got to the bottom of Tanner's Hill, instead of turning up the road, towards Wellbeloved Café, they crossed over and headed down Deptford High Street instead. The open-air market was in full swing, with traders calling out their wares and greeting the women warmly.

Before too long, they rounded the corner onto Douglas Way. The busy market continued, stalls lining both sides of the street. A pleasant hubbub accompanied the sight. But as they manoeuvred between shoppers, another sound reached Baz's ears.

Oh no, not again.

Because, of course, Mitch and his pals were near the

entrance to the Albany Theatre, making a nuisance of themselves. As usual.

'Well, lookie here.' Mitch pointed at the women as he bellowed, 'If it ain't Blue Hair and Pronouns. One'll run you down with her hagmobile and the other will pervert your kiddies!'

Baz felt her chest tighten. Despite the cool, fresh air, she feared she might faint. But Peggy didn't hesitate, ploughing right through the centre of the group, causing several of them to leap out of her way at the last second.

Baz stayed as close behind Peggy as she dared. As they passed Mitch, Peggy whispered, 'Crispin.'

Mitch's face blanched and he vibrated with rage. If looks could kill, Peggy's heart would have certainly stopped. He looked like he could murder someone right there and then.

What Mitch *didn't* do was ask Peggy who she was talking to or what she meant. He definitely didn't ask her to repeat herself. 'C'mon, lads.' He pointed further along the crowded road and told his gang he thought he spotted ... Baz couldn't bring herself to repeat his language even in her own head. The group moved like a swarm of angry hornets.

Carole and Madge caught up with Baz and Peggy just in time to head into the theatre.

Inside, they were met by Paul and a man who looked vaguely familiar. It took Baz a moment to realise he was the man who kept trying to talk to them.

'Oh, loves!' Paul ran over to them. 'Just park your scooters here, next to the door. Were those brutes giving you a hard time again? I'm so sorry – I promised the girls I'd keep an eye out for you but I got chatting to...' The way Paul pointed at his companion made Baz suspect she wasn't the only one who couldn't remember the man's name.

The man stood watching Paul, seemingly unaware of the

growing awkwardness. He tossed a ring with dozens of keys, spinning them around and around on his finger.

She still couldn't remember his name, but Baz did recall that he was the one who had ... unusual proclivities. 'Warm in here.' She shuddered.

Madge unzipped her coat. 'We know Arthur.'

That was the fellow's name.

'Do you? Lovely.' Paul clapped. 'He's just been telling me about his battle with the council. He's trying to persuade them to build a new wildlife park in the area.'

That didn't sound right to Baz. Arthur looked like he wanted to correct Paul, but didn't get a word out before Paul continued. 'But of course, you know the council. They're more concerned with— Well, I'll be honest – I have no idea what sorts of thing the council's senior leaders worry about. I know it isn't libraries or community centres.' He turned and flapped a hand at the much-taller Arthur. 'Did I tell you I work for the community centre?'

Once again, Arthur opened his mouth to speak but Paul had already turned towards Baz and her friends.

'So, ladies,' Paul continued without even pausing for a breath. 'Any progress to report in our missing persons case? Come on, spill the tea. I *need* to know everything!'

'Oh, good lord,' said Peggy. 'I need a drink. Come on, Carole, love. Let's go see if we can rustle up a coffee.'

Arthur blinked. 'Someone's gone missing?'

'They have indeed!' Paul splayed his fingers and touched his chest. 'And our friends here are playing Miss Marple, doing a bit of investigation into the mysterious case of the vanishing queens.' He made jazz hands when he spoke the last few words.

Arthur looked puzzled. 'Will the show go ahead if one of the queens is missing? It's not Bluebird is it?'

Paul playfully swatted Arthur on the arm but it was Madge

who replied. 'It's not one of the queens from today's show. Clive — do you know Clive?'

Arthur shook his head.

Madge carried on regardless. 'Anyhow, Clive asked us to look into the disappearance of his friend Eddie.'

Arthur was studying Madge. 'Eddie?'

Hands still swinging wildly, Paul looked at Arthur. 'She means Sue. You remember Sue — Sue Panova? She performed with Royal Tea sometimes. Her boy name is Eddie. She vanished, oh ... almost three weeks ago now.'

Baz was starting to feel like a third wheel in this conversation. She wished she had something to contribute.

'Oh dear,' Arthur said. 'I hope everything's all right. But I'm sure the police are doing all they can.'

Madge kissed her teeth. 'The police? Arthur, you know better than that. What do the police care about a missing asylum seeker?'

'They, erm, they ran a task force,' said Baz, finally feeling like she had something to contribute.

Both Paul and Arthur looked at her, eyes narrowed.

'They did what?' Paul's eyes opened wide and he touched his chest. 'I can't believe I didn't know about this!'

'I don't understand,' Arthur said. 'If she's only been missing a few weeks, when did the police run a task force?'

'That's the thing.' Baz leant a bit closer to the men. 'It's not just one missing person. There are—'

'Yoo-hoo! Wagwan, ladies?'

Madge's face was impassive. 'Clive.'

Coco Celeste touched her chest and made a show of looking to her right and then her left. 'Who is this Clive you speak of? I don't know anyone by that name. He sounds dreadfully dull if you ask me.'

Baz kissed Coco's cheek. 'I didn't realise you were part of today's show.'

Coco nodded politely. 'I am, darling. Can't get rid of me that easily.' She looked at Madge again. 'But since you mentioned our *mutual friend* Clive — however tedious the man is — he did ask me to pass along a message.'

Madge arched an eyebrow. 'And what's that?'

'He wanted me to thank you for sending that delicious mountain of a man to assist with his immigration foibles,' replied Coco.

Madge crossed her arms over her chest. 'For pity's sake, Cl — Co— Ugh. Just speak plainly.'

Coco closed the space between Madge and herself and took Madge's hands in her own. 'Thank you.'

Madge looked like she might say something dismissive. But then she just nodded.

Coco took a step back and put her hands on her hips. 'Also, Blue sent me over to say the show's going to be starting soon, so you should probably take your seats.'

Baz looked around for Peggy and Carole. But Madge took her arm and guided her. 'I don't know why that horrible man is always asking so many questions.'

'What?' Baz took her seat next to Carole and then turned around. 'Which man?'

But as they took their seats, the show started and Baz never did hear Madge's response.

CHAPTER 14

in which truffles steals the show

THERE WAS no wind and the sun was shining brightly as the four women made their way up Brookmill Road. Despite appearances, Peggy fought a shiver.

The only question was whether their quarry would be home. But, of course, Madge knew one of the neighbours. Was there anyone in this blasted corner of London she didn't know? She'd pumped her friend for details of the man's habits and had been reliably assured that he was normally home of a Sunday afternoon.

Thankfully, they passed the bloody nature reserve without running into that tedious bore, Arthur. At the next street along, they all turned right. It was a bland, unassuming street lined with bland, unassuming, flat-fronted Victorian terrace houses.

When they arrived at their destination, Baz and Peggy parked their scooters. Baz whispered, 'It's not exactly what I expected. Looks like a million other houses in London.'

Peggy gave a slight shrug. She was well aware of how deceptive appearances could be.

Madge pressed the bell. This was followed immediately by a frantic, high-pitched barking. She bent and pushed the letter box open, shouting through it. 'Hello, Mitch.'

Footsteps could be heard on the other side of the door and a man's voice muttered, 'I'm coming – keep yer hair on.' When the door swung open, Mitch stood inside, cradling a small white fluffy dog in the crook of his left elbow. 'You. What do you lot want? Come to attack a poor old man in his home? Maybe you'd like to kick little Truffles here while you're at it.'

Peggy sneered. 'Don't be ridiculous. I wouldn't dream of hurting *him*.'

Once they'd discovered the man behind the CCTM property empire, Baz had made easy work of finding his addresses. He had several of them, but the women guessed he'd base himself at his London home when he had protesting activities to keep him occupied. The carefully gleaned information from his chatty neighbour had confirmed that assumption.

Madge squared her shoulders. 'Aren't you going to invite us in?'

Mitch shuffled his position so he towered over Madge. 'No.'

Peggy shifted into position next to Madge. 'Oh, I think you're going to want to hear what we have to say.'

His lip curled. 'You ain't got nuffink I wanna hear. And I ain't having none of yous in my house. You're not my kind of people, see.'

Peggy had left her old self behind many decades ago. Her accent wasn't that much different to what it had once been – but her manner, her way of speaking, her way of presenting herself to the world were what had really changed. She drew on the airs of that long-ago Peggy and endeavoured to channel her younger self.

No. Not her own past self. Pulling herself up to her full height and lifting her chin, Peggy channelled her mother, with all the hauteur that implied. Her voice dropped slightly in pitch as she added a touch of gravel and a more nasal tone. Her words came quickly – but gracefully so. 'I don't know, Crispin. I really think you ought to hear us out. Only we've come all this way, you see, and I'd hate for us to have to go away and enact our plan B. And I really do believe, honestly, that our little proposal is a mutually beneficial one.'

'Don't call me that,' he growled. He wouldn't look her in the eye.

She made a flicking motion. 'Come on, stand aside. Let us in and we can get the unpleasantries out of the way.'

Mitch took a long, slow breath – all the while snuggling the small dog in his arms. 'Fine. Suit yourself. Ten minutes. But you betta make it worth it.' He ushered the women into a tastefully appointed living room, that smelt of a herbal, woodsy air freshener.

Baz leant in close to Peggy and whispered, 'Where on earth did you learn to do that?'

Peggy shot her friend a warning look. 'Later.'

Mitch settled himself in a pale blue velvet armchair, resting his right foot on his left knee. He set the dog on the floor and made a vague gesture that seemed to indicate the women should – or at least could – seat themselves wherever they liked.

Peggy sat on the sofa, next to Carole, who immediately opened her knitting bag and removed a mitten she'd been working on. She settled in and got to work, ignoring everything and everyone around her.

Peggy rubbed her thumb and fingers together and Truffles approached her cautiously, sniffing her. The dog permitted her to rub his ears. After a moment, he turned and leapt up onto Mitch's lap, perching on his knee.

'What is it you fink you know?' Mitch scooped the dog up and pulled him to his chest, like a tiny, furry shield. The sharp sounds and guttural tones of his words were at odds with the genteel surroundings.

'Oh, we know quite a lot about you,' said Madge from her perch on an upholstered ottoman in the bay window.

Mitch stroked the dog's ears. 'Well then. You know more 'an me. As always with you lot, it seems.'

Peggy affected a look of surprise. 'Oh, did you want to know about us, Crispin? All right. My name is Peggy – that's Margaret Persephone Trent, daughter of Maude Wolston Trent, Baroness Bromley. Ah, that rings a bell, I see. Yes, I thought it might – you do seem like a Tory.'

Peggy placed her hand atop Carole's. 'And this is my lesbian life partner, Carole.' She motioned towards Madge. 'This is my friend Madge. She's a nurse – and an immigrant. And, as you can plainly see, she's also a woman of colour.' She paused for a breath. 'Finally, this is Baz. She's a transgender woman. Oh, and a forensic accountant.'

Her introductions had been calculated. The women had discussed them in advance. They wanted to see how he'd react.

Mitch didn't bat an eye – at least, not until the last revelation. She'd been wondering how much of his own rhetoric he really believed. Not much, she suspected. He just didn't care.

'So, that's us,' Peggy continued. 'And then there's you. Does everyone call you Mitch? Or only the people you're using to stir up hate and division?'

Mitch pulled the dog even closer and jabbed his thumb in Baz's direction. 'What? So only some are allowed to change how they identify? I fot you people believed in free expression.'

Peggy smiled coldly. 'You're free to be who you are. That's why I asked if everyone calls you Mitch. If Mitch is who you are, then fair's fair. But I don't like people who show one face to some people and an entirely different one to others. So, I ask again, are you Mitch or are you Crispin?'

'All right.' Crispin/Mitch shifted in his seat. When he spoke again, his voice was different. Like Peggy, he could shift both his accent and manner of speaking as easily as most people change shoes. 'Think of it this way. Mitch is ... a character I play. He's useful. Just like these drag queen friends of yours, I have a persona I can put on and take off. Most people in my daily life call me Spino, as it happens.'

Peggy snorted. 'And what would your little group of friends think if we were to introduce them to Spino, I wonder?'

Spino puckered his lips. 'That's your threat? Because, honestly, I think they'd survive. If you want me to leave your *friends* alone, you're going to have to do better than that.'

Something about his threat left Peggy fighting a shudder.

Madge motioned at Baz. 'Go on, dear. Tell the man what you learnt.'

'Erm.' Baz licked her lips as she smoothed the papers on her lap. But then something changed in her. She straightened her back. Peggy suspected she was doing a shift of her own: from a person who so often doubted herself into a law enforcement professional accustomed to questioning perpetrators of financial crime.

Baz lifted her chin. 'Are you familiar with the Rise and Shine Day Nursery on New Cross Road?'

Mitch responded with a move that was part shrug, part defiance. But there was a darkness in his fair eyes.

Baz gave a crisp nod. 'Right. The nursery in question mainly serves low-income families and the owner is barely scraping by. Despite this, she's been advised that her rent will be doubling, which will push her out of business.'

'Don't see wha's got to do wiv me,' Mitch said, returning to the charade of being a working-class lad from *sarf-ees* London.

Smoothing the papers again, Baz continued. 'My friends and I took an interest in the case. In particular, I did some research into who the landlord might be. Unfortunately, this particular building was owned by a very complex web of shell companies, many of which are domiciled in tax haven jurisdictions.'

Mitch seemed to notice Baz for the first time. He studied her. 'So?'

Baz studied the man right back. Peggy saw in her the relentless pursuit of justice that had always driven her.

'So,' said Baz. 'I'm sure you're aware that tax evasion is a crime. Specifically, we're talking about the crime of "cheating public revenue", the maximum sentence for which is life in prison or an unlimited fine.'

A heavy silence blanketed the room for several heartbeats.

Baz scratched her ear. 'It took quite a lot of digging to get to the truth in this case – a phenomenal amount of effort. Whoever constructed this web...' She sighed and shook her head. 'Hats off to them, really. It's a masterful piece of work.'

Baz rested her hands on her knees. 'But my team and I, you see, we're better.'

Spino's face remained neutral. 'What do you mean?'

Baz thumbed through the papers until she found the one she was looking for. 'It took a lot of effort. But eventually we were able to unravel it. CCTM Holdings.' She chuckled and looked up at Mitch. 'You really are a brazen little miscreant, eh? CCTM. Crispin Caspian Todd-Mitchell. Truffles Developments.' She gestured at the dog in his lap. 'It took me ages to untangle your warren of companies within companies.'

Spino rubbed his chin. 'So I have good financial advisors. What's your point?'

Baz was in her element – Peggy had never seen her look so confident, so comfortable in her own skin. 'No, Mr Todd-Mitchell. A *good* advisor would ensure you pay precisely your fair share of taxes – no more, no less. A dubious financial advisor would help you avoid taxes you would otherwise owe. But one who helps you commit tax evasion? Well, that's an advisor who'll end up in the neighbouring cell to his clients.'

Inwardly, Peggy was cheering for her friend.

Spino's skin blanched. 'You've got no proof.'

'Do I not? Oh, dearie me. I was sure I had...' Baz ran her finger down the page in front of her, then turned the page and repeated the process. 'Oh, yes. That's a relief. All here.' She lifted the pages up and held them out. 'Would you like to see?'

He stood up and snatched the papers from her and returned to his chair, still clutching Truffles to his chest.

Cocking her head slightly, Baz smiled. 'That's just one copy, of course. There's another on my desk, in an envelope addressed to HMRC. My granddaughter will drop it in the post first thing tomorrow.'

Mitch growled and the little dog scarpered. In a single graceful leap, he bounded from Mitch's lap to Peggy's.

The dog weighed virtually nothing – but beneath all the fluffy white fur, he was all sharp angles and pointy bits. Peggy released an involuntary *oof* when he landed. No one else seemed to notice. She stroked his soft fur.

Mitch rubbed his face. 'What d'you want?'

'There's a good lad.' Madge nodded approvingly.

Baz smiled. 'My friends and I have a business proposal for you. I think you'll find it mutually beneficial for all parties concerned.' She drew in a breath and pulled herself up straight. 'That is, all except His Majesty's Revenue and Customs – it distinctly lacks any form of benefit for them. Though I don't suppose there's any need to tell them, now, is there?'

Mitch appeared to have frozen. He sat stock still, not even breathing for a moment. 'Go on.'

Peggy rubbed the dog's ears – Cookie was going to be so jealous when she got home.

'Two things,' Baz said. 'Firstly, you will sell two of your properties to me – for a very reasonable price, of course.' She indicated Madge.

Madge acknowledged Baz then turned to Mitch. 'We had our solicitor take the liberty of drawing up the contracts. Your solicitor should find everything in order.' She reached into her bag and pulled out more papers. She stood up and walked the papers over to him.

He studied the papers, flipping through all the pages. His lip curled into a sneer. 'A reasonable price, eh? Those properties are worth five times that.'

'Mr Todd-Mitchell,' Baz said. 'I made some estimates on the back taxes you might owe on these two properties alone. Not to mention the prison sentence, of course.' She smiled. 'I think you'll find we're being more than generous.'

He pressed a finger to his temple. 'What's the second thing?'

Peggy stroked Truffles. 'Oh, that one's easy. Won't cost you a penny.'

He looked at her, and there was something vicious in his eyes.

'You leave Royal Tea's shows alone.'

Mitch tapped his chin. 'Just me?'

Peggy winced as the dog jumped off her lap and returned to Mitch. 'Without the head, we think the snake will probably ... find something else to do with its afternoons.'

Baz licked her lips. 'Have your solicitor look over the paperwork. I'm sure they'll agree everything's in order. You have forty-eight hours to accept. If I don't hear from you within that timeframe, that letter will be delivered to HMRC.'

Mitch shook his head and got to his feet. 'I fink your time is well and truly up.'

Baz got to her feet, standing straighter than Peggy had ever seen her. 'Mr Todd-Mitchell, it's been a pleasure doing business with you.'

Mitch ushered the women out of his house as quickly as possible and slammed the door so hard the vibrations made Peggy's teeth clatter.

'Drat,' said Carole. 'I never even got a chance to use my knitting needle.'

CHAPTER 15

in which the tea is spilt

PEGGY PUSHED the grey-green door open and was rewarded with a blast of warm, fragrant air. Once they were inside, Carole and Cookie indulged in a simultaneous shake to rid themselves of the fat raindrops that clung to them. Peggy grunted a greeting at Sarah and continued into the second room.

They all said their hellos as Peggy doffed her coat and hung it on one of the hooks behind Baz. She accepted Carole's coat from her and hung it up next to the others.

Baz looked up from her embroidery. 'You're lucky you only caught a few seconds of that.'

Peggy grunted as she took her seat.

The bell chimed as the door opened again. Peggy groaned when a now-familiar face appeared.

Paul folded his umbrella and unzipped his raincoat, revealing a colourful bow tie. 'Morning, ladies. I'll just pop to the front and grab a cuppa before I stop for a chat.' He frowned. 'Er, can I get anyone anything?' He put his coat on the back of a chair, which he dragged over next to Baz's – the presumptuous git.

Baz winced as she stabbed herself with her needle. 'Oh, that's very kind. Thank you, Paul. Our drinks are on their way already.' She held her hand in an awkward position – apparently endeavouring to simultaneously avoid dripping blood on her handiwork and hide the injury from Paul. She failed on both counts – judging both by his look of horror and Baz's frantic dabbing at the embroidery once he'd left.

There was something off about the man; why did he keep showing up? Why was he so interested in the case? He didn't seem to be particularly close to Eddie.

Judging by how jittery Baz got whenever he was around, Peggy wasn't the only one who mistrusted him. She considered the matter as she opened her bag and pulled out her laptop. Trying not to re-read the words she'd written last night, she flexed her fingers a few times before resting them on the keyboard.

Will crossed his arms over himself. 'Don't try to deny it, Kitty. I saw you. I saw you with him with my own two eyes.'

Kit touched a finger to Will's chest. 'Me? With Ben Jonson? Surely you jest, Will! I'd sooner eat my own shoes. You know how I detest him. Surely you've mistaken me for someone else.' A cheeky grin spread across his face. 'Maybe you've tripped and fallen into one of your own plays.'

A few minutes later, Paul walked through the open doorway

into the café's second room, bearing a tray heavily laden with teapots and cups. 'All righty. Sarah sent me through with your drinks. Let's see what we've got here.' He set his burden down and picked up a ceramic teapot. 'These two are both breakfast tea. One for you, my lovely.' He placed the pot in front of Baz with a coy smile and then picked up the identical pot. 'And one for Carole.'

Peggy waved him away impatiently. 'We're perfectly capable of sorting ourselves out.' She snapped up her espresso. As she gave it a quick stir, she breathed in the aromas: dark chocolate and caramel being the dominant ones.

When they'd all settled themselves and fixed their beverages to their liking, Peggy leant back in her chair. 'Paul, why are you here?'

Paul plucked a speck off his knee and dropped it to the floor, where it was promptly inspected by Cookie. 'Right. Of course. I should be respectful of your time. This is mainly a social call. But of course I also wanted to see if there's been any progress in the case. The ... er, the missing people. I, er...'

Peggy's teeth were starting to grind.

Madge pulled her glasses down her nose and peered at Paul. 'You've taken a great deal of interest in this case.'

'Oh, yes, absolutely.' Paul clapped. 'I mean, these poor people had no one to look after them. Nothing's being done – not by the police at any rate. What a shame – so sad.'

Madge breathed slowly. 'Yes, yes. We know all that. What I mean is ... we've spoken to quite a few people over the past few weeks. People who know Eddie, Wilson, Fifi, and the others. You – as near as I can tell – don't really know any of them.'

'Oh, I knew Eddie.' Paul nodded vigorously. 'And I'm sure I saw Fifi perform a time or two. I'm not sure I knew her to say hello in the street but—'

The door chime jangled and two familiar figures walked in. Paul didn't seem to notice and kept blithering. One of the newcomers headed to the front counter, but the other ducked his head and came to join the women. At this rate, they'd never have a chance to discuss what progress they'd each made the night before.

'Morning—' Alas, Peter didn't get any further than that.

Paul glanced up and then several things happened all at once. He released a shrill squeal before clambering out of his chair with no grace or dignity, knocking it over. His tea spilt. Baz's croissant fell to the floor. Thankfully, the plate didn't break – but the croissant disappeared under the table in suspicious circumstances. 'Sorry, I just remembered ... a thing ... I have to...' Paul ran out the door, crying.

Peggy cast a glance at Madge. *That wasn't suspicious at all*.

'Well.' Peter bent to pick the plate and coffee mug up off the floor. 'Was it something I said?'

'I...' Baz began. But then her voice trailed off. She scratched her head.

Peggy shrugged. 'I've no idea what just happened but I think this is the best thing that's ever happened to Cookie.' The dog had finished his unexpected treat and emerged from under the table, where he licked up the remnants of Paul's tea.

Madge pulled her glasses off and let them hang from the beaded chain around her neck. She looked up at her grandson. 'Good morning, Peter.'

Uh oh. Peter was in trouble now. Madge subscribed to the view that the person arriving owed the people already present greetings and not the other way around.

Peter shook his head like he was trying to clear it. 'Sorry, sorry. Good morning, Granny. Good morning, Aunties.'

Peggy grunted at the young man. Ever since he'd joined the Met, Carole mostly refused to acknowledge Peter.

Baz's good knee bounced as she said hello. Peggy assumed

she was worried about the instruction to stop investigating the case.

Peter smoothed his short dark curls. 'Listen, about the other day. I'm really sorry. My sergeant asked me to have a chat with you off the record. It wasn't my idea. Actually, I, er, I begged her to send someone else instead... But she said it had to be me or else it would have to be on the record.'

Madge reached out and patted Peter. 'You're a good boy, Peter. I know you'd never disrespect your elders like that unless someone forced your hand.' She put her glasses back on.

He looked at Madge. 'You're not playing investigator anymore, right? You stopped like ... they asked, yeah?'

Madge put on her most solemn expression and nodded. 'Of course, Peter.'

Baz coughed and Peggy shot her a look. 'I hope you're not coming down with something, Baz.'

Madge pulled a pack of throat lozenges from her bag. 'Pass these to Ms Spencer, would you please?'

Baz accepted the cough sweets from Peter without looking at him. 'Thank you.' She studied her fingers carefully as she unwrapped one.

'Now.' Madge set her bag back down. 'To what do we owe the pleasure of your visit this morning?'

Peter chuckled. 'Oh, nothing really. Keeley's a bit of a coffee snob. She says you've got the best coffee in all of Lewisham. I think she'll be dragging us in here pretty much every shift.'

Madge's eyebrows arched. 'While the young woman is undoubtedly correct, you shouldn't need her to give you a reason to come see your granny.'

Peter looked like he wasn't sure what to say, but just then his partner appeared at his side and offered him a reusable cup. 'Morning, ladies. How's everyone doing?'

'We're all fine, thank you,' said Madge. 'Keeley, right?'

When the officer nodded, Madge continued. 'I hear I have you to thank for this Monday morning visit from my grandson.'

'Well...' Keeley smiled a dimply smile. 'Training's been rough. PC Ibeh's a great teacher and all ... but it feels like I'm constantly running to keep up with him. He makes everything look so easy. So when I saw how much he squirmed last week when he had to warn you off an active investigation... What can I say?'

After a quick glance at Peter, Keeley cleared her throat and raised her coffee mug. 'Er, that is, Sarah makes a fine cup of coffee. I think you'll be seeing more of us in here.'

'Thank you,' said Madge. 'We use an award-winning local roastery. But the barista's techniques and the equipment make a significant difference.'

Keeley tilted her head and bit her lip.

Peter looked at her and rolled his eyes. 'Oh, didn't they tell you? This isn't just my grandmother's favourite café, it's a family affair. Granny and her friends co-own it.' He waved in the direction of the main room laconically. 'And that's my auntie Sarah at the front counter.'

Keeley tossed her hands in the air. 'Even better. We're not just supporting an independent local business – we're supporting your family. Win-win!' She punched him in the arm, then turned back to the women, flashing a high-wattage grin. 'With that, I think we'll take our leave and get back on the streets, where we belong.'

Madge looked at her friends. 'Well now, what in heaven's name was that all about? With Paul, I mean.'

'It was bizarre.' Peggy frowned. 'What an odd little man.' An idea had been flitting around in her brain – but just out of her reach. It was so close, she could feel it.

Madge shook her head. 'Very much so. And why is Paul so

interested in what happened to these missing people? At every step of our investigation, he's—'

Baz slapped her embroidery down into her lap. 'I cannot believe the pair of you.'

Peggy exchanged a glance with Madge. 'Baz, what on earth are you talking about?'

Baz drew in a breath but her face was getting redder by the second. 'You, Madge. Not five minutes ago you promised that lovely young man that we wouldn't interfere with an ongoing investigation. You looked him right in the eye and swore to him that we were no longer looking into the missing persons cases.'

Madge kissed her teeth and looked away.

Peggy bit her lip to keep from chuckling but Baz rounded on her. 'And you, Peggy. How dare you! That man has been unfailingly kind to us. He's been nothing but lovely since the moment we met him. You have been rude and abrupt and sarcastic. And why? Because he's taking an interest in the disappearance of some vulnerable people caught up in suspicious circumstances? That's all it takes to make you suspicious?'

Peggy inhaled sharply as the idea finally snapped into place.

Madge cocked her head. 'What's that?'

'I've just realised something.' Peggy tapped her chin. 'Paul. Something about his manner has always struck me as odd. I've finally figured it out. It's not only that he keeps wanting to worm his way into our investigation despite not knowing any of the victims very well, he's also the only one who consistently refers to all the missing people in the past tense.'

Madge looked at the ceiling. 'Hmm. That is odd.'

The four women sat in silence for a few minutes. Peggy had to admit, the signs were starting to point the same way. She watched out the corner of her eye as the flush slowly drained from Baz's face.

Eventually Baz pinched her lips together. 'Why was Paul so afraid of the police?'

'Mmm hmm.' Madge carried on knitting.

Baz swallowed. 'And if Paul's so concerned with the welfare of the missing people – as he claims... Then why hasn't he reported their disappearances to the police?' Her hand was trembling.

Peggy was warmed by the pride she felt as Baz started asking the important questions. 'Why indeed?'

Madge looked up and frowned. 'I think it's time we pay a visit to Paul.'

Baz's cup rattled as she poured herself more tea. 'Erm.' She took a breath. 'I trust we've all learnt our lesson about accusing someone without hard evidence? You know ... last time?'

Peggy paused. 'We will go prepared for any outcome. But, yes, Baz.' She nodded at her friend. 'We will ferret out the truth before we ... take action. I promise.'

CHAPTER 16

wherein misunderstandings abound

BAZ STUDIED herself in the mirror and swallowed.

The concierge locked eyes with Baz's reflection. 'Everything all right there, Ms Spencer?'

Am I all right? Baz honestly didn't feel qualified to answer. Running her fingers over her hair, she studied her reflection.

She wondered what Paul saw when he looked at her. If he was behind all the disappearances, she didn't fit the pattern. She was a UK citizen after all. She may have only recently moved back, but she had been born in this country and spent her first twelve years here. Unlike the others, she also had family and friends who wouldn't hesitate to report her disappearance to the police.

Not that she was about to go missing.

That wasn't on the menu for today. Though a confrontation was. The butterflies in her stomach wouldn't let her forget that.

'Shall I call an ambulance?' The concierge put a gentle hand on Baz's shoulder.

Baz was jerked from her reverie. 'I'm sorry, Jessica.' She

shook her head, trying to clear the cobwebs away. 'I was miles away. What were you saying?'

Jessica bent close and looked in Baz's eyes. 'I'll say you was. You got off the lift and then you just ... stopped. Honestly, I thought you was having ... one of them whatchamacallits.' She made a loose gesture. 'Absence seizures. My little sister used to have them when we was kids and I swear our mum was convinced she was faking until...' She waved her own words away. 'Sorry, you don't need to hear my family history. What matters now is ... are you okay?'

Baz smiled at the young woman. She was the one who'd helped Daisy after she'd fought off her attacker a few months before. Baz owed this woman a great deal. 'Sorry. I assure you, I'm fine. I promise. Just, well, I suppose my head's in the clouds. I'll be fine – I promise.'

Jessica cocked her head. 'You sure?'

Baz was grateful for Jessica's concern. 'I'll be fine.' She motioned towards the tower block's front door. 'The fresh air will do me good.'

Jessica sneered. 'If you can call London air fresh, I guess.'

Baz smiled again, feeling genuine warmth for this lovely young woman. 'I'll be fine. Thank you for your concern.'

Nodding, Jessica pressed the button to open the front door. Baz waved and then squeezed the scooter's accelerator.

Outside, her thoughts threatened to overwhelm her once again. She allowed them to flow as she wheeled down the road, but reminded herself to pay attention to where she was going.

These poor people – seven that they knew of – had met some sort of nefarious end, she was sure of it. At the hands of...

That was the question, wasn't it?

The light turned green and Baz steered into the intersection.

All signs pointed to Paul. She wasn't *so* enamoured of him

that she couldn't see that. But the fluttering in her chest reminded her that she had been sweet on him. Or was she still?

Baz felt a jolt tear through her as her scooter mounted the lip of the kerb on the far side of the road. As she rounded the corner, Madge came into view. She was alone at the bus stop. A bus pulled over and the door opened. Although she couldn't hear what was said, it was clear that Madge was conversing with the driver.

As Baz grew closer, the driver waved. 'See you around, Mrs Dixon.'

Madge nodded. 'Thank you, Tommy. You look after that ankle.'

When the bus pulled off, Baz said, 'Afternoon, Madge.'

'Good afternoon.' Madge turned to face her. She made a show of looking at her watch. 'Nice of you to be on time.'

Baz smiled and motioned in the direction the bus had gone in. 'Friend of yours?'

'Tommy was one of my patients,' said Madge. 'Quite a complex fracture. Needed an ORIF. He was in hospital for several days. Terrible traffic accident.'

'Oh.' Baz studied her friend. 'How long ago was this?'

'Let's see.' Madge looked up and to the left. 'Had to have been 2013.'

Baz's eyes opened wide. 'And he still remembered you?'

Madge looked indignant. 'Of course.'

'Look.' Baz pointed across the street to where Peggy and Carole were waiting for the light to change.

The women weren't taking the bus; it was merely a convenient place to meet. Once all four were gathered, they set out, walking north on Church Street. After a few minutes, they reached their destination: a four-storey red-brick block of post-war flats.

Peggy leant her head back, gazing up at the block. 'If you

tell me we're climbing all those stairs, he can jolly well come down here to us.'

Baz breathed slowly. 'It's a ground-floor unit – but Paul did warn me there are a couple of steps at the entrance. He suggested we leave the scooters by the pram stores.'

Peggy harrumphed, 'Just as soon as we find those.'

Once they found the pram sheds, the four women approached the building, looking for flat number four.

When they arrived at the yellow door, Baz reached out to ring the bell. Her adrenaline was spiking and her bladder desperately wanted to release its contents.

Behind the door, a cheerful voice called out, 'Coming, love!' When the door swung inwards, Baz caught a glimpse of Paul's face in the instant before his delight turned to confusion. 'Oh. Ladies?' He looked at Baz. 'What ... what's going on?'

Baz forced a cheerful grin onto her face and tried to will herself to mean it. 'Hello, Paul. I'm not sure what you mean.' She couldn't help but swallow. 'I did say we should talk. And here we are. To talk.'

Paul straightened his bow tie. 'Well, yes. But I thought you said *we* should talk.' He waved back and forth between the two of them. 'I didn't think you meant *we* were going to talk.' His hand moved in a circular motion, indicating all five of them.

Baz's chest tightened. She needed a drink – a good strong cup of tea. This was it: the moment he'd either invite them all in or Madge would push past him and make the decision for him.

Time seemed to have frozen. Her heart thumped a staccato beat inside her. But after a few seconds, Paul stood aside and swung the door open wider. He was wearing an apron festooned with kittens and rainbows. A sweet, smoky scent filled Baz's nose. 'Then I suppose you'd better come in. I'll put the kettle back on and make another pot of tea. The one I, er...

The one I've got out is only... That is, it isn't big enough for all of us.'

He ushered the women into a narrow hallway and then into a small living room. 'Just through here, please.' Soft music was playing but he hustled to an ancient-looking device and switched it off. The fireplace looked like it had been closed off, but a cluster of candles burned in its place – presumably the source of the pleasant aroma.

'Oh, er, I—' He pressed his lips together. 'It's a bit draughty in here, so I put some candles on. I can blow them out if you like – I should blow them out.' He moved past the women.

Peggy dropped into place on the sofa. 'It's fine.'

Paul nodded – just a few too many times. 'Please seat yourselves. Anywhere you like. Er, there's not really much space. I should grab another chair or two. I think I've got some somewhere.'

Carole walked up to Paul. 'It's lovely to meet you, George.' She took his hand and pulled him close. Baz could barely make out the words she whispered into his ear. 'I've been hoping to make your acquaintance. I need to tell you about what goes on at the equator. Have you been south of the equator, George?'

'It's Paul.' He looked like he was struggling to get Carole to release his hand. 'And I'm afraid I haven't.'

Carole released him and laughed – a loud, bawdy sound. She winked. 'Well, then what kind of prostitute are you, eh, George?' She stepped carefully over nothing and joined Peggy on the sofa.

Paul stood blinking in the centre of the room, looking like he might cry.

He pointed at the room's sole upholstered armchair. 'One of you two should sit. I'll make more tea and fetch some chairs.' He touched a finger to his lips. 'I'll see if I can't rustle up some— Some tasty little treats too.'

Madge stepped forwards. 'Baz, you should sit before your knee gives way. Paul, you needn't worry about goodies. We've come prepared.' She indicated the wheeled shopping bag she'd been pulling, then put a hand on his elbow and steered him from the room.

Baz realised Madge had been right: her knee was growing weak beneath her. Mind you, at that moment, there wasn't much of her that didn't feel weak. She couldn't identify the complex mêlée of emotions coursing through her. Her throat was closing, the room was uncomfortably warm, and her stomach was leaden.

'Oi.' Peggy was waving her cane in Baz's direction. 'Do what the nurse ordered before you faint. We don't want to have to carry you out of here.'

'Does Baz need a lift?' Carole was on her feet in a split second. She wrapped her arms around Baz. Baz made to do as instructed and sit down – but Carole had too strong a hold on her.

Peggy rolled her eyes. 'Put her down, love. I meant we'd have to carry her if—' She waved. 'Never mind. Just let her take a seat.'

The three women sat quietly for several minutes. Beyond the walls of the living room, dishes clinked and doors creaked. Something made a horrible squeaking noise. Baz was about to ask if they needed a hand when Paul appeared in the doorway, dragging a battered office chair – the source of the squeak. The chair had castors, but one of them wasn't turning.

'There we go,' Paul said. 'Everyone all right?' He waited for them to nod then departed again.

A minute later, he carried in a small square table. 'I'll be fine on this. Back in a tick.'

When he returned, Madge accompanied him. Paul held a tray with two teapots and an array of mugs and assorted dishes.

Madge bore the cupcakes she had made. They laid everything out on the coffee table.

'Now, Peggy,' Paul said. 'Madge tells me you don't drink tea. She suggested I make you a coffee.' His eyebrows climbed to the very top of his face. 'I've only got instant, so I made you a cup of that. Much as I do love the coffee they serve at your lovely little café, it's a bit out of my reach, I'm afraid.' He handed her a mug of coffee, then set about pouring tea into the remaining mugs.

Madge waved at a stack of small plates. 'I've made cupcakes. And there are some biscuits.'

Baz spied a plate with two flower-shaped cookies with a circle of jam in the centre. A flash of guilt ran through her as it occurred to her that Paul had probably purchased these for their ... meeting. When he thought it would be just the two of them.

She breathed a silent prayer, pouring every fibre of her soul into the words. *Dear God, don't let it be him.*

Paul looked at her with his beautiful golden-brown eyes. And then he looked down at the Jammie Dodgers. She smiled at him and reached out to take one of the biscuits. The grin he looked back at her with made her grip the arms of her chair with knuckles as white as the bone beneath the skin.

What if it was him? Her stomach tightened and she wasn't sure she could eat the cookie after all. *But surely, if it was, it's better to find out now than to fall under the spell of those eyes?*

Once everyone was settled with food and drink in hand, Madge opened the conversation. 'Paul.' His eyes moved as though through treacle as he turned from Baz to Madge. 'I'm sure you can guess why we're here.'

Paul swallowed. 'It's about the case.'

Peggy took a long drink of her coffee and then set the mug on the table. 'It is.'

The silence hung in the air in much the same way that teapots don't. Eventually, Paul said, 'Go on, then. Don't keep me waiting. What have you discovered?'

Madge plucked a bit of fluff from her sleeve and deposited it in her pocket. 'We have discovered a number of disappearances, stretching back many years – all of people affiliated with the LGBTQIA+ community.' Madge spoke the initialism slowly, as though she had to remember what each letter stood for. 'And all of people facing immigration challenges.'

Madge raised a brown stoneware mug to her lips and took a drink. 'I admit I was reluctant to see a pattern. It has been my experience that sometimes people who are experiencing difficulty with our immigration system are less rooted to the community. People are sometimes driven underground, whether through fear or in search of opportunity. It shouldn't be that way – but it is.' She breathed slowly. 'However, I have been persuaded to see this as a pattern. We believe these people have come to harm.'

Paul looked down at the floor, his face a complete blank.

'Seven people have gone missing,' Baz said. 'Hassan Abbas, Samuel Musa, Abdullah Sultana, Moses Okello, Fifi Galore, Wilson Joseph, and Edvin Marku.'

Paul didn't move. He didn't even appear to breathe.

'Shall we tell you what we've noticed?' Peggy sat with perfect posture, looking positively regal. When Paul didn't respond, she continued. 'We've seen *you*, Paul, taking an interest in all of the missing people – not only the ones you know personally but all of them. We've seen you popping up at every stage in our investigation. And – this is one I find especially interesting – at every stage of this investigation, you've referred to the missing individuals in the past tense. To someone paying close attention, it appears as though you have information no one else does.'

For a moment, nothing happened. And then Paul looked up. He stared at Peggy. 'Of course I have information no one else does! And, yes, I am 100 per cent confident that every single one of them is ... dead.' His voice broke on the final word and it came out as nothing more than a mouse's squeak.

'You...' Baz's heart fell out through the soles of her feet. She couldn't believe it. But she had to.

CHAPTER 17

in which more tea is spilt

PAUL REACHED into his pocket at the same time as Carole reached into her knitting bag. Baz knew exactly what she carried in there. And she never wanted to see anyone die ever again. No matter how desperately the killer of so many people deserved to die.

'Don't you understand?' Paul pulled his hand from his pocket and all four women were braced to act – not that Baz had the slightest clue how she was meant to act when faced with an armed serial killer.

But all Paul held was a tissue. When he dabbed his eyes, the women relaxed a bit.

A bead of sweat dripped from Baz's forehead onto her cheek. 'Don't we understand *what*, Paul?'

'It's not seven people.' A small sob escaped him. 'It's eight – if you're right about all the people you discovered. What was the first name you mentioned?'

'Hassan.' Baz breathed the name. 'Hassan Abbas.'

Paul wiped his eyes with the tissue. 'And when did he go missing?'

'May 2015,' Peggy replied.

Paul shook his head, tears still flowing. 'He wasn't the first. He couldn't have been. Because there was someone else in 2014.'

A few heartbeats passed before he spoke again. 'A sweet, beautiful, wonderful man. We were going to be married, you know. Equal marriage was brought in in March of that year, you see. Only we had to wait until his asylum application was processed.'

Baz had so many questions, but the one that escaped her lips was, 'Why did you have to wait?'

Paul laughed sadly. 'It's the immigration rules. You're not allowed to marry in this country until both parties have leave to remain. I couldn't sponsor him as my income was too low. So we had to wait for his asylum case to be settled. We were due to go to the Home Office in May, but he ... went missing in April.'

He wiped his eyes again. 'My Pius. He wouldn't have left me, you know. He wouldn't have.'

Madge's eyes were wide open. 'Pius?'

Paul nodded and then blew his nose noisily.

Madge held herself very still. 'Pius Birungi?'

Paul sat upright. The two of them stared at one another for what felt like an age.

'You knew him?' Paul looked incredulous.

Eventually, Madge shook her head. 'He didn't go missing. He got a job opportunity in Liverpool. Nothing to do with this case.'

Paul looked at Madge, a deep frown creasing his face. 'Liverpool?'

'That's right.' Madge's voice was firm, sure of itself. 'For work.'

Baz looked around for a box of tissues. Finding none, she went in search of the bathroom.

From the living room, Paul's voice reached her ears. 'Who on earth told you that?'

As there were no tissues in the bathroom, Baz grabbed the loo roll and rushed back.

'How did you even know him?' Paul accepted the roll from Baz, electricity coursing through her as their fingers brushed. 'Thank you, dear. That's very kind.' He dabbed at his cheeks with the toilet paper.

'He lived with me.' Madge looked almost lost for words – an unusual state of affairs indeed.

'You?' Paul studied her for a moment. 'You were his landlady, host, whatever you want to call it... That was you?'

Madge nodded. 'For eleven months. And he didn't even tell me when he left.'

Paul burst into laughter, which swiftly turned to tears. 'He was so afraid of telling you he was gay. Told me you were "a nice church lady". We argued about it. I said if you couldn't accept him, he could find a new host. That if you kicked him out for his sexuality, then you weren't very nice after all. But he was so secretive and fearful.' He dabbed at the fresh tears rolling down his cheeks.

Madge's face fell. 'Pius ... is gone?' She began wringing her hands. 'I never...' Her chin dropped to her chest and her shoulders heaved.

Paul got up off the table he sat on and knelt in front of Madge, taking her hands in his own. 'Who told you he left?'

Madge's lip quivered. 'I... I can't recall.' She shook her head. 'I wish I could remember but I can't.'

Peggy inhaled and then breathed back out slowly. 'Well, then. Whoever told you he went to Liverpool knows something that will shake this case open.'

Paul pulled himself awkwardly back to his feet. He scratched his head. 'Hang on.' He shuffled backwards until his little side table connected with the back of his knees. Dropping onto its surface, he looked at Baz. 'You're here because ... you thought ... I was—'

He burst into tears again, looking like he was about to collapse back to the floor.

Baz went to him, touching his shoulder, steadying him. 'We didn't know. And I certainly hoped not. But you have to admit, there were signs that you knew more than you were letting on.' She chewed on her lips. 'And what was that business with you running out of the café like that, anyways?'

Paul raised his head but kept his gaze focused on the floor. 'There were cops. I might have panicked. A bit.' He chuckled. 'I suppose that did look awkward – didn't it?'

Madge scowled. 'That was young Peter, my grandson!'

'Ah.' Paul's light brown skin flushed. 'I'm sorry. I'm a poor, queer, Black man. I've got a record – all activism-related, innit? Nothing like... You know. The cops – as a rule – don't particularly like people like me. And the feeling is generally mutual.' He looked at Madge. 'Sorry, no offence. I'm sure your grandson is a wonderful man.'

Madge nodded.

Paul's eyes lit up. 'Oh, if you want final proof it couldn't be me... I was out of town the week Eddie went missing. I went on a little holiday down to Brighton. Stayed with a friend. I have pictures on my phone if you want to see.'

He stared at the floor, looking like he wanted to say more. 'Actually...'

The women looked at one another as Paul ran from the room. An inner door opened and rummaging could be heard. A few seconds later, he returned with a picture frame. He turned it to face them. 'Pius.'

The image showed a younger Paul embraced by a much taller, larger Black man. Both men grinned so broadly that Baz's heart soared – until she remembered.

A tear fell from Madge's eye as she reached out. 'Pius.' The two hugged and let their shared loss bring them together for a few minutes.

Baz clasped Paul's hand. 'Thank you.'

Peggy stood up. 'This has been most insightful. But it's time for us to go.'

Carole frowned. 'But I didn't even get to use my knitting needles!'

CHAPTER 18

in which madge runs away

TWO WOMEN and their dog stepped out into the bright late-January sun. It was chilly despite the clear sky. As soon as the light hit Peggy's eyes, she flinched. 'Ugh.'

Carole touched her elbow. 'Is it the Etruscans again? I told Tony Blair – that prick – that if he showed up here again with that lot, I'd be ready for him. Where's my knitting needle?'

Peggy raised a hand. 'We're safe. From both ancient superpowers and former Prime Ministers. At least for the time being.'

'Thank heavens for small mercies,' Carole replied. 'What's got a dachshund in your boxers then, love?'

Peggy opened her handbag and retrieved what she needed. She smiled as she flashed the case at Carole. 'Sun's out. Need my shades.' She popped the small round lenses on before slipping the case back into her bag. 'Ready?'

'Like a tiger.' Carole nodded.

The short walk took a ridiculously long time because Cookie insisted on stopping to sniff every blade of grass, every fence post, and every bit of rubbish along the way. But eventually, they arrived. Baz's scooter was already parked out front.

Just as Peggy was about to push the door open, a voice called from her left. 'Yoo-hoo! Wagwan, ladies?'

Peggy turned to find Clive racing down the street towards them, running with his chest out and elbows aloft.

'Clive,' Peggy said through gritted teeth.

Carole held out a hand, holding it up like she expected him to kiss her ring. 'Good morning. I'm Alice Morgan, a research scientist whose parents were brutally murdered.'

Clive waved her away melodramatically. 'Yeah, yeah. And I'm the queen of England.'

Carole stopped and stared at him. Peggy assumed she was about to call him an idiot.

But then Carole did something that surprised her. A broad grin spread across her face and she punched Clive on the shoulder. 'That's right – you are.'

Clive rubbed at his shoulder. 'Ow! What'd you do that for?'

Peggy shook her head. There was no winning with some people. 'You two can stand out here and quarrel all you like. Cookie and I are going inside where it's warm.' She pushed open the door and made her way in. Unsurprisingly, Carole and Clive followed.

Peggy grunted a greeting at Olena before heading into the second room – where she found that tedious man sitting in her seat yet again. 'Arthur.' She thumped the leg of her chair with her cane. She might agree with his aims in keeping the council's hands off that nature reserve, but that didn't mean he wasn't a wearisome bore. When he made no move to vacate her place, she added, 'Come on. Off you pop.'

Arthur pulled himself to his feet. Peggy waved away the proffered papers before he could open his mouth. 'Yes, yes, you can leave some leaflets or petitions or what have you.' She made a shooing motion. 'Now off you go. Lovely to see you and all that. Goodbye.'

Peggy lowered herself onto the finally vacant chair.

Arthur nodded repeatedly, almost to himself. 'I bid you ladies, ah, good morning.' He turned and shuffled through the doorway to the main room. When he was gone, Baz looked up from her embroidery and smiled. 'Morning, Peggy. Lovely day, don't you think?'

Peggy pulled her bag onto her lap and retrieved her computer. 'What in heaven's name has you so cheerful?'

Baz's ruddy skin flushed easily, but it was Madge who answered. 'Apparently young Barbara here is relieved to discover her paramour is innocent.'

Peggy screwed up her face. 'What? That funny little man we visited yesterday?' Baz's face grew even redder – though the Lord alone knew how that was possible. Peggy rested the computer on her knees and folded her arms. 'Explain.'

'I rang him last night.' Baz touched a finger to her hair, sweeping it behind her ear.

Peggy cocked an eyebrow. 'After we accused him of being a serial killer?' She dropped her voice on the last two words. Even she didn't want anyone to overhear their suspicions.

'After.' Baz pressed her lips together, smearing her lipstick. 'We had a good long chat. He apologised for not telling us about Pius. And I apologised for ... for, well ... you know.'

'And?' Peggy didn't understand the appeal of men. Obviously, she couldn't write the stories she did without at least some hypothetical understanding. But to her, the attractiveness of men had always been a sort of distant, theoretical knowledge. Fictional men could be attractive – at least to other fictional men. But real men? No, thank you.

'Don't turn your nose up like that, Peggy.' Madge shook her head.

'And what?' asked Baz.

Peggy lifted the lid of her laptop to wake the device. 'And are you going to see him again?'

'Oh.' Baz grinned as she looked down at the floor. 'Yes, actually.'

Peggy looked at her friend. 'You're not going to cook for him, though, are you?'

Baz's mouth fell open. An indignant look flashed across her face before she burst out laughing.

'Wagwan, ladies? What's so funny?' Clive's return interrupted their laughter. 'Sorry it took so long to get my coffee but the girl asked me to wait until your drinks were ready.' He set the tray down.

Peggy took a deep breath. 'Clive.'

Clive distributed the pots and mugs before dragging a chair over so he could sit with them. 'Also that lovely friend of yours was there to chat with while we waited to place our orders.'

Peggy scowled. 'What friend? What on earth are you on about, man?'

Clive lifted his coffee to his mouth but didn't drink. 'Why Arthur, of course. He said you'd been helping him with his campaign to save the nature reserve. He's even offered to take me up there tonight. It's not open to the public, you know. But he's the caretaker, so he's got the keys, of course. We're going to make a little evening of it.'

Madge's face fell slack. She lifted a hand to her mouth, swallowing as she did so. The colour drained from her face, leaving her washed out and ashen.

Peggy didn't know what was going on in Madge's head, but she'd put money on the idea that something had just clicked into place. 'Clive. It's been lovely seeing you. Thanks for stopping by. Now take your cue and – not to put too fine a point on it – get out.'

Baz, too, seemed to have noticed something was up with Madge. 'Erm, yes. Thank you, Clive. We'll be in touch as soon as we have more info about your missing friend.'

Clive screwed up his face and kissed his teeth. 'All right, all right! A girl can take a hint. There's no need to be so rude.' He stood up, grabbed his coat, and flounced out of the room. A moment later, the bell on the front door jangled more harshly than necessary and the door slammed shut.

'Well,' Baz said.

Peggy nodded. 'Madge, what is it?'

'Keys.'

Peggy exchanged a glance with Baz. Apparently she didn't understand the reference either.

Peggy studied Madge. 'Madge, what keys? What do you mean?'

'I've just...' Madge stood up, dropped her knitting summarily into her carpet bag, and bustled out of the café. A moment later, she could be spied outside the window practically running up the road.

Peggy shrugged, palms upwards. Baz looked back at her and shrugged. 'I suppose we ought to follow her?'

Peggy slammed her computer shut. 'I suppose we must.'

The women set about gathering up their things. Peggy picked up her coffee and gave it a quick swirl. She swallowed the shot, barely noticing the notes of cherry or demerara sugar. 'All right, let's be off.'

Peggy pulled open the front door. After collecting Baz's scooter, the three women and Cookie headed up the hill. They could see Madge's rotund shape in the distance. She was nearly at her building.

It didn't take long to get to Madge's place. Although climbing the stairs to the first floor was a challenge for both Peggy and Baz, they made it with a minimum of fuss.

Madge's red front door hung wide open. Peggy stopped on the threshold and knocked anyway.

'Through here,' Madge called. Peggy followed her voice to the living room. Cookie wagged his tail and smiled as he approached Madge. She was standing at the dining table, a banker's box in front of her.

Madge stopped to give Cookie a cuddle before returning her attention to the box. She lifted the lid off and began retrieving items. Greeting cards, letters, children's drawings. Madge pointed a finger in the air, vaguely indicating the kitchen. 'Go and fetch some tea – would you?'

Peggy shook her head and huffed. She pointed Carole at the sofa and left Cookie with her. Of course, Cookie knew where the treat jar was and was instantly fussing at Carole to give him one.

Peggy beckoned for Baz to follow her to Madge's kitchen. 'We'll put the kettle on.'

'There's cake in the cupboard,' Madge called from the other room. 'May as well bring us all some of that while you're at it.'

Peggy stepped into Madge's small kitchen and got to work.

'Oh my!' Baz hovered in the doorway. 'Madge does all her cooking and baking in here? How on earth does she manage it? There's no counter space.'

Peggy wagged a finger at her friend. 'Careful. Your privilege is showing.'

She didn't need to turn around – she could envision Baz's face flushing with embarrassment. 'Oh, yes. I suppose it is.'

Peggy pulled down the teabags, instant coffee, and cake from one cupboard. 'The kitchens on this estate are all this size. People make do.' She pointed. 'Teapot and cups are just there if you would. And the little plates, too.'

As she removed spoons from the drawer, she heard Baz open the cupboard. 'You used to live upstairs, didn't you?'

Peggy pulled the serving tray from its place between the oven and the fridge. 'Straight above. Carole and I were there from 2015 to 2020, when my body decided a ground-floor flat was crucial.'

Baz put the dishes on the tray on the hob, then handed Peggy the teapot and one mug. 'So you never knew this Pius character?'

Peggy poured water into the teapot and the mug with the instant coffee. 'No. We weren't far away before that time but I didn't meet Madge until after we moved in. Right, have we got everything?'

Baz nodded. 'I think so.'

Peggy bobbed her head. 'Well, then. I guess we'd better see what's got this bee in Madge's bonnet.'

When they crossed the hall to the living room, they found Madge and Carole seated together at the dining table. The banker's box had been relocated to the floor, but Madge held a single sheet of torn paper. Peggy set the tray down on the dining table and Baz followed with the teapot.

Peggy and Baz took their seats.

Baz gestured at the teapot. 'Shall I be mother?'

Madge nodded, so Baz poured three cups of tea as Peggy served up plates of Madge's homemade rum cake.

Madge wrapped her hands around her mug of tea, but there was a hint of a tremble in her friend's normally rock-steady hands.

Peggy drew her mug of coffee towards herself. 'All right, then. Spit it out. Whatever you've got to say, you know we can deal with it.'

Drawing in a breath, Madge sat up straight. 'I know who the killer is.'

Peggy made a *go on* gesture. 'Don't keep us waiting.'

Smoothing the paper out in front of her, Madge kept silent

for a moment. Peggy could see faint pencil marks on the paper, but couldn't read the words.

'Something Clive said this morning jolted my memory,' Madge said.

'You think *Clive* is the killer?' Baz's words were little more than a whisper but they still stopped Madge in her tracks. She glared at Baz.

Baz winced. 'Sorry, sorry. Please go on.'

Madge pursed her lips. 'He mentioned keys. It triggered something in my memory – a man jostling a set of keys as we spoke.' She touched a finger to her temple. 'I needed to find this note.'

Peggy bit her lip to stop herself from shouting at Madge to get to the point.

'In April 2014, I was working at Lewisham Hospital,' Madge said quietly. 'When I arrived home one evening, I found a note from Pius.' She caressed the paper in front of her. 'He said Arthur was going to show him the nature reserve.'

'Arthur!' Baz's hand shot to cover her mouth. 'Sorry, please go on.'

Madge held the paper up to her nose. 'Dear Mrs Dixon. I'll be home late tonight. Arthur has promised to show me the nature reserve. It's not open to the public, but he has the keys. He needs my help with some maintenance. Yours in Christ, Pius.'

She set the note in the centre of the table. The women sat silently for a few moments, digesting what they'd just heard.

Peggy eyed Madge suspiciously. There had to be more than this.

Baz raised her eyebrows and spoke slowly. 'And *this* is what made you think Arthur was the killer?'

Madge's head snapped to look at Baz. 'This? By itself? No.

But a few days later I spoke to Arthur. You know he lives in this building, right?'

Peggy nodded and Baz shook her head. Carole studied her spoon.

'He does,' Madge said. 'Just a few doors along. Anyhow, I hadn't seen Pius since the day he'd left that note. I told Arthur I was worried.' She paused. 'I remember he was holding those keys of his. He has one of those keyrings: the kind with a thousand keys and no way to differentiate them. He was toying with it — spinning it around on his index finger, then tossing and catching it.'

Madge paused and the room was perfectly still. 'When Clive mentioned going to the nature reserve, I just...' She shook her head. 'That image came back to me with crystal clarity. Over and over in my head, I can see him tossing those keys and catching them. I remember what the air felt like that day, the noise the keys made. I can't tell you what I was wearing or where I was going. But those keys, I can see and hear them clear as day.'

'What did he say?' Baz's voice was soft but urgent, like she didn't want to interrupt Madge's reverie but had to know the rest.

Madge held herself still for a moment, then looked at Baz. 'I asked Arthur if he'd seen Pius. And he apologised, told me this was the first chance he had to pass along a message. He looked me in the eye and said, "I ran into him on the stairwell on Tuesday morning on his way to the station. He said he'd been offered some under-the-table work in Liverpool. He asked me to tell you he was sorry for leaving so abruptly but he didn't want to miss out on the opportunity."'

Peggy waited to be sure Madge was finished speaking. 'On Tuesday. He definitely said on Tuesday?'

Madge nodded.

Baz tapped the note on the table. 'What day did Pius leave his note?'

Madge looked down. 'It's dated 15 April 2014. Because I worked such unsociable hours, we always dated our notes. Sometimes we went a few days without seeing one another.'

'What day of the week was that?' Baz asked.

Peggy pulled her computer out. It took only a moment to determine that the fifteenth had been a Tuesday. 'Madge, do you remember anything about that day? I know it was a decade ago, but the more detail you can remember, the more certain we can be.'

Madge stood up. 'Let me get my diary.' Because of course Madge would keep a decade-old paper diary of all her daily activities. Of course she would.

She left the room, returning a moment later with a coil-bound notebook, thumbing through the pages as she walked. 'Yes, here we go – 15 April 2014. I worked the overnight shift. Got home at nine. Pius made breakfast for us both. When I got up later, that's when I found his note.'

Madge waved the diary. 'How did I never put this together? Pius couldn't have left on Tuesday morning – I was with him on Tuesday morning.' She paced the room.

Baz screwed up her face. 'Maybe you misremembered. Or he misspoke. It doesn't mean...'

Peggy tutted. 'Oh, come on. Pius didn't go to Liverpool for work. Just like the others didn't. The only possible reason for Arthur to make up such a cockamamie tale is because he knew Pius wasn't coming back.'

Madge resumed her seat and caressed the note. 'He's taking people to that nature reserve and killing them there. It's the only explanation.'

Peggy sighed. 'Someone needs to ring Clive.'

Baz furrowed her brow. 'Clive?' She gasped. 'Oh!'

Madge nodded. 'Oh. We need to get Clive away from that man. But also, we have no idea how long Arthur spends grooming his prospective victims or preparing for them. Will he simply find another victim or will he try to persuade Clive to meet with him at a later date?'

Frowning, Peggy rubbed her nose. 'We're going to have to act quickly.'

CHAPTER 19

wherein carole gives a grammar lesson

IT WAS chilly as Baz made her way along New Cross Road. It had gone 10 pm and the temperature had fallen below freezing. It's never truly dark in London, though, thanks to the light pollution. The moon was past full – a waning gibbous phase. She crossed Brookmill Road and then turned up the intersection before the one that would take her to Wellbeloved Café.

She thought about the last time she'd come this way late at night. She'd been on her way to tell Peggy that they'd got it wrong. Not Daisy – but she and Peggy. An innocent man nearly lost his life because of their assumption. That wouldn't happen this time.

Before long, she arrived at her destination. She parked her scooter in the forecourt and made her way to the front door. Her heart was in her throat as she pressed the button.

The speaker crackled to life with Peggy's voice. 'Is that you, Baz?'

'It's me.'

The buzzer sounded and Baz pushed open the door.

She heard the door to the flat swing open before Carole's

head popped out. 'Oh, Baz. What a lucky coincidence. I've been meaning to talk to you about the nuclear testing. You know about the *tests* they've been running in Windsor since 1913 – don't you? It's all Theresa May's doing.'

Carole swung the door wide to let Baz enter. Though, of course, Cookie was blocking the path.

Baz held out her hand. 'I have to pass the sniffspection first, eh?'

Carole made shooing motions at the dog. 'The Rebecca Riots passed him by. He still thinks the gatekeeper is entitled to set whatever toll they like.'

Peggy's voice sounded from the other room. 'For heaven's sake. Are you lot going to spend all night chatting in the corridor or are you going to come in and join us for dessert?'

Baz removed her shoes. She'd worn slip-ons specifically to facilitate the easy on-offs she suspected she would need this evening.

In the living room, Cookie clambered back onto his favourite chair. Carole was taking her seat at the dining table.

Peggy was around the corner in the kitchen. 'Will you take coffee, Baz?'

Coffee? At this time of night? 'I wouldn't want to be up all night. Oh, but then there's a possibility we're going to be up half the night anyways, isn't there? Go on, then. Yes, please. Thank you.'

Peggy stuck her head out of the archway to the kitchen. 'You're out of luck on that front – it's decaf.'

Baz remembered Peggy once telling her she always drank decaf. Something about caffeine giving her gas?

Peggy emerged from the kitchen with a serving tray bearing a French press and three mugs. 'I had a bell from Madge earlier. Here, I need the tray back if that's okay.'

Baz took the tray and carried it to the table. 'Oh, right?

What did she say?' She transferred the coffee and mugs to the table, then handed the empty tray back.

Peggy returned a few moments later, having reloaded the tray with plates of cake and cutlery. 'She spoke to Clive. Sure enough, the day Eddie went missing, he was due to go on a date in a park. Clive didn't know who with but he was sure the name started with A. I wasn't sure how you took your coffee, so I brought some milk and sugar.'

Baz took a seat at the table. 'Are you seriously thinking of eating now? At this time of day?'

Peggy threw back her head and guffawed. 'We've only just finished our dinner.'

Having supper at 10 pm? Peggy really was a night owl!

Pouring coffee from the French press into three mugs, Peggy gave a small shrug. 'You can have the slice of cake or we can let Carole and Cookie fight for it – your call.'

Carole accepted her coffee and stirred four heaping spoonfuls of sugar in. Then she glanced at the snoozy German shepherd with his head hanging off the armchair. 'I can take him.'

Baz took a small sniff of her coffee. 'Oh, that's good stuff.' She added some milk and then took an exploratory sip. 'Excellent.'

Peggy nodded. 'It's from the same roastery the café uses. As a little thank you for making the connection, my nephew sends me a bag every week.' She waved. 'A thank you, a Christmas gift... I'm not really sure anymore *why* he sends it. But he does.'

Baz held the mug. 'Your nephew?' This was new territory. 'I don't think I've ever heard you talk about your family before.'

Peggy chuckled. 'You heard the bits I told that mendacious turgid toad. But, no, I suppose I don't speak about them much. Alex is all right, but I don't get on with most of them – least of all my mother.'

Baz tried to think of how to respond to that.

'My mother and I have never seen eye-to-eye.' Peggy tapped a nail on the table. 'She's a dyed-in-the-wool Tory, you see. And not a "namby-pamby, liberal, one-nation Tory" – her words, not mine.'

Baz scratched the back of her head. She must have misheard. 'I'm sorry, did you say she *is* a Tory?'

Peggy nodded. 'She is indeed. The last time I spoke to her, she went on at me about how we haven't had a proper Tory PM since Thatcher. She had no kind words to say about ... well, about anyone. She went off about the invasion of the Woke Brigade. Apparently they're taking over the country.' Peggy pulled a face like she'd tasted something bad – which certainly wasn't the coffee.

'Your ... mother?' Baz still couldn't wrap her head around the idea.

'Oh, do keep up, Baz.' Peggy sliced a bit of cake off with her fork and popped it into her mouth. 'Ninety-seven years old and I don't think she's missed a week at Parliament since 1986.'

'Your mother is ninety-seven?'

Peggy stabbed a morsel of cake with her fork and jabbed it in Baz's direction. 'Are you having a stroke? Only having to call an ambulance would throw a bit of a spanner into our plans.' Peggy's mobile phone trilled and she held it up. 'Looks like it's go time. Better postpone your stroke and get your head screwed on straight.'

Madge had invited Arthur round to hers for a *date*. Seeing as he had a sudden change of plans when Clive cancelled.

Peggy popped an earbud in and clicked the face of the phone. 'How are you getting on, Madge?' There was a pause while, presumably, Madge spoke. 'Excellent. We'll see you then. My what? Ah, excellent thinking. Okay, I'll bring it.' She slid the phone back into her pocket. 'We'll need to leave here in about twenty minutes. Let's see if we can clear up some of this mess before then, shall we?'

'We're not leaving for twenty minutes?' Baz was aghast. 'What? Why?'

Peggy picked up the plates and mugs and carried them through to the kitchen. 'How should I know? Grab that French press, would you?'

Baz dropped her voice – though she wasn't sure why. 'What's she doing? We should help her. Is she just sitting there with him tied to a chair or something? We need to go now.'

Peggy set the dishes in the sink and turned on the tap. 'If Madge wanted us to come now, then that's what she would have said.'

'What about Roshan and Ara?' Madge's tenants shouldn't see what they'd be getting up to tonight.

Peggy made a shooing motion. 'They're out for the night. Now go on, get out of our way.'

Carole tapped Baz on the shoulder. 'I wash – Peggy dries. Otherwise it takes her weeks to figure out where I've hidden everything.'

'What?'

Peggy took Baz by the shoulders and turned her around. 'We've got this. You go and keep Cookie company. He likes it if you read to him. We've been working our way through the latest Dharma Kelleher novel. It's on the coffee table.'

Baz went back into the living room. 'Looks like it's just you and me, kid.' Cookie wagged his tail. She sat on the armchair – his chair. He plonked himself down on her feet and rested his chin on her knee. She stroked his soft fur while she waited for Peggy and Carole to tidy up.

For pity's sake... She had to get her head together. Absent-mindedly stroking Cookie, she stared at nothing.

Once Cookie had been delivered to the upstairs neighbours, the three women set out.

Peggy affixed a trailer to her scooter. 'I don't need it very often, but every once in a while, it comes in handy. I got it a few years ago when Cookie hurt his knee and I was taking him to the vet all the time.'

Baz steered her own scooter out Peggy's front gate. 'And this is what Madge asked you to bring? Why?'

Peggy barked out a laugh as she followed Baz. 'I think I can guess.'

Baz swallowed. She'd made peace with the unpleasant nature of the work they sometimes did. But she didn't like to think of it any more than necessary.

As she dismounted her scooter, Baz braced herself for the laborious climb up the flight of stairs.

Peggy surprised her, though, by walking right past the stairwell. 'We're in luck. Madge said the lift's working for a change.'

It creaked and groaned like it was going to crap out on them at any moment, but it eventually got them to the first floor, where they found Madge's door ajar. 'In here.' Madge's voice came from beyond one of the doors in the short hallway. That door, too, was open.

Peggy pushed open the door, revealing Madge in a neat but cramped bedroom. And laid out on the bed was Arthur. Madge was fussing with one of his socks. His other foot was bare.

'All right,' said Peggy. 'Cavalry has arrived. What's the status?'

Baz peered around Peggy's shoulder. 'How long has he been unconscious? We ought to tie him up before he wakes.'

Madge retrieved a sock from her pocket and pulled it onto his left foot. When she had finished, she stood upright and faced the women at her door. 'He's not going to wake up – he's dead.'

Peggy marched into the room. 'He's what?'

Baz followed Peggy, but with less strident steps. She felt like she ought to check the man's pulse – but she knew Madge, as a nurse, wouldn't look kindly on being second-guessed.

'I said he's dead.' Madge crossed her arms over her chest. 'And I think you heard me the first time.' She manoeuvred a dilapidated trainer onto his foot.

Peggy stepped right up to Madge and stared down at her. 'Madge, what the hell are you doing? Did you really take on a serial killer by yourself?'

Baz made a conciliatory gesture. 'We don't know that he's ... that he was a...'

Madge arched an eyebrow. 'Oh, yes we do.' She waved a gloved hand at her nightstand before setting to work on Arthur's second shoe. 'I found that in his flat.'

Peggy touched her fingers to her temples. 'You went to his home?'

Baz narrowed her eyes. 'How did you do it?'

Madge pointed at Peggy. 'Yes, but not until afterwards.' She redirected her hand so she was pointing at Baz. 'Potassium chloride. It will appear he had a heart attack.'

'Wouldn't that be...' Baz scrunched up her face. 'Why would he eat something that tasted so strange?'

Madge arched an eyebrow. 'Have a look at that paper I found on his fridge-freezer.'

Baz cocked her head. 'Will it tell me why he willingly ate something so salty?'

Peggy donned gloves and picked up the paper. She studied it for a moment, her eyes growing slowly wider. After a moment, she touched her mouth. 'Oh.'

Madge had finished putting shoes on the corpse. She stood up straight, then pushed her fists into her lower back and arched. 'Indeed.'

Baz wagged a finger. 'No, I'm sorry, please. I need an answer. How did you manage it?'

Madge snickered – actually snickered. Peggy cast a sideways glance at her and opened her eyes wide.

But Baz was still in the dark and she didn't like it. 'Please, Madge. How did you manage this?'

'Well...' Madge had a coy look on her face. 'The normal method of administering potassium chloride would be intravenously.'

'Okay.' Baz nodded slowly. 'So you injected him.'

Madge looked away. 'A puncture wound would show up in even a cursory post-mortem. And that leaves us with absorption via mucosal membrane.'

Baz threw her hands in the air. 'I don't understand. Can you just explain, please?'

Madge and Peggy exchanged one of those infuriating glances.

'Baz,' Peggy said, drawing the name out. 'I think – and I'm going out on a limb here but... How shall I say this?' She did that teeth-kissing thing that Madge always did. 'Baz, don't ask questions unless you're sure you want to know the answer.'

Baz furrowed her brow. 'But I *do* want to understand.'

Madge bit her lip.

Peggy inhaled slowly. 'I'm not sure you do.'

'A colon is nearly always preceded by a complete sentence.' Until Carole started speaking, Baz hadn't even realised she was in the room. 'And in its simplest usage, it rather theatrically announces what is to come.' Throwing back her head, she laughed uproariously.

Baz felt heat run to her cheeks. 'Are we talking about an S-E-X thing?'

Peggy gave a tiny shake of her head and frowned. 'Baz, W-H-Y A-R-E W-E S-P-E-L-L-I-N-G?'

Baz looked at the floor as she fought the urge to flee. After a moment, she shook her head and waved. 'Fine. I don't want to know. Now what's on this paper you've been waving around?'

'Gloves on.' When Baz had done so, Peggy offered her the page. 'It's a hand-drawn map of the nature reserve.'

Baz studied it. The walking path was clearly marked, as were the toolshed and the entrance. But the map had also been flagged with eight small red circles, each one labelled with a letter of the alphabet. She spied an F first. When she noticed a cluster together with S, M, and A, she realised what she was looking at. 'Oh my gosh.' She traced a finger around the page looking for... Yes, there was the E. It took her just a few seconds to find the P, H, and W.

Baz let her hand fall to her side. 'He's buried them in the nature reserve.' She looked up to find Peggy and Madge's eyes on her. 'That's what this is, right?'

'Yes.' Madge's earlier coquettishness was gone. She spoke plainly now. 'I have a plan. And it's why I asked you to bring the trailer.'

'I think I see where this is going,' Peggy said. 'Let me see that map again.'

Baz passed it over.

Peggy held the map up and indicated the circle with the F. 'Fifi's grave is closest to the entrance. I say we work with that.'

CHAPTER 20

in which a corpse is paraded through london

AN HOUR LATER, they left Madge's flat with a large, heavy parcel wrapped in rubbish bags and an old duvet. Carole carried one end of the bundle and Madge the other.

When they'd made it as far as the lift, Baz went down first to serve as lookout. Once she was on the ground, she rang Peggy. 'The coast is clear.' She could have shouted, but they were trying to avoid calling attention to themselves.

As the lift door was about to slide open again, though, a young man appeared.

'Oh, er, good evening.' Baz wasn't sure whether she was speaking loudly on purpose or if she just couldn't help it. 'Sorry, I didn't see you there.'

The man nodded in greeting and looked like he was about to head off. When the lift door scraped open, Baz let out a startled squeak. She hoped it wasn't audible – but it almost certainly was. Maybe it blended in with the noise of the door. She could only hope.

'Evening, Aunties. Oh my days. That looks heavy. Here, let me help you.'

'You,' screamed Carole. 'You get your hands off my soufflé. I know my rights. You're not taking me back to your secret underground laboratory.'

Madge's voice was calm, measured. 'Thank you, Damien. That's very kind – but as my friend says, we're perfectly capable of carrying our parcel. Perhaps you could just assist Peggy in bringing the trailer over.'

'Oh, er, yeah, sure. Of course.'

Baz held her breath. Why were they letting this innocent young man help them dispose of a dead body? What on earth was Madge thinking?

Peggy and Damien headed towards where she'd parked her scooter. 'I think, Damien, how we can best use you is if you hold the trailer steady while Carole and Madge – that is, Mrs Dixon – load the bundle into it.'

'Of course, yeah.' Damien nodded before jogging back over to where Madge and Carole were awkwardly emerging from the lift with their burden. 'Hey, are you sure I can't help you, Mrs Dixon? It don't feel right – me standing here watching you carry that. Looks heavy, innit?'

'It's fine,' grunted Madge as Peggy reversed into position. 'You just steady that trailer for us, Damien.'

He grimaced but did as he was told.

When the women deposited the corpse into the trailer, a trainer-clad foot dropped out and hung at an odd angle. Baz shuddered and released a small but – she felt sure – fully justified shriek.

Damien didn't seem to notice the human foot. Instead he looked at Baz. 'You sure you're okay, Auntie? Do you need me to call someone for you?' He rubbed his neck. 'Or maybe get you something?'

Baz tried to swallow down her rising panic and focus on remaining upright despite the fog of dizziness that threatened to envelop her. 'I'm fine. I'm fine. Sorry.'

Peggy waved in Baz's direction. 'Don't mind Baz. She's a nervous Nellie.'

His hand still on the back of his neck, Damien looked down at the bundle in the trailer. 'Oh my days, Aunties. That's gotta be well heavy! You shoulda let me carry it for you.'

'Young man, I could benchpress you, I'll have you know,' said Carole. She leant in close to him and whispered, 'I terrify my personal trainer.'

Damien laughed nervously. 'I'll bet you do, Auntie.' He rubbed the back of his curls. 'What's in it anyway?'

All four women replied at the same time.

'Carpet,' said Baz.

'Dog food,' said Peggy.

'Compost,' said Madge.

Carole smiled brightly and clapped. 'It's a dead body. Would you like to see?'

Baz winced. They should have got their stories straight before leaving the flat.

But Damien held his hands up in self-defence. 'All right. My bad. You're right – it's none of my business.'

Madge tucked Arthur's leg back into the trailer with no visible sense of shame. She dusted herself off and looked up. 'Thank you, Damien. We appreciate the assistance. You may go now.'

Damien waved cheerily as he set off. Baz watched him bound up the stairs to the left of the lift, taking them two at a time.

Despite the chill of the night air, Baz had to wipe sweat from her brow before it dripped into her eyes. 'That was close.'

'What in heaven's name was all that screeching about?' Peggy turned to face front. 'No, never mind. Let's just get this thing done. Everyone ready?' Without waiting for an answer, she squeezed the accelerator on her handlebars. And then it was Peggy's turn to let out an involuntary cry as the scooter rolled backwards. Apparently the mobility scooter couldn't handle the heavy load combined with the car park's steep incline.

Baz, Madge, and Carole all ran towards her, reaching out to stop the scooter from rolling back. 'I think if you turn, Peggy,' Baz said, 'you should be able to leave at a less steep angle. And with our help, you should be able to get moving. Once we get onto the road, it's downhill and then level, so you should be okay.'

With Baz, Madge, and Carole all pushing Peggy's scooter from behind – not that Baz imagined her strength added much to the mix – they eventually got Peggy moving. Baz returned to her own scooter and soon the women were on their way.

They passed a man cycling a zig-zagging path the wrong way up the one-way street. 'Evening, ladies. Bit nippy out tonight, innit?' he slurred.

'Oh, George.' Carole waved at the man to stop. 'I keep meaning to tell you... We really do need to talk about what happened in Majorca. You remember – with the Pope and that pop singer?'

'Stupid bitch,' muttered the man, trying to steer his bike away from them and only barely succeeding. 'My name's Stanley and I ain't Catholic. As you well know!'

Carole turned and shouted at his receding back. 'Everyone knows that bears strictly follow the catechism.'

Baz felt a rush of relief course through her as they got moving once again.

They turned onto Albyn Road, a small residential street that would take them most of the way. They had almost a kilometre to traverse. Given the late hour, Baz hoped they'd be lucky enough to avoid any further interactions with people.

Alas, it wasn't to be. As they crossed Friendly Street, someone shouted, 'Oi!'

'Just ignore him,' Peggy said. 'He'll give up.' The women kept on moving. But the man chased after them. Baz noticed both Carole and Peggy put their hands into their pockets. Madge reached into hers too, but a troubled look crossed her face when she did so.

'Oi! Excuse me.' The man was gaining on them.

When Baz had told people about her plans to move from Edmonton back to the UK – and more specifically London – her colleagues, friends, and family all expressed concern that she would be the victim of serious crimes. They all seemed convinced that south-east London was some sort of haven for violent thugs and criminals of all sorts.

Baz cast a glance at the deceased serial killer in Peggy's trailer and willed his ghost to shut up just as the shouting man caught up with them and laid a big beefy hand on Madge's shoulder.

CHAPTER 21

in which a shocking discovery is made

PEGGY'S HEART leapt into her throat. Without taking her eyes off the man, she caught a glimpse of Carole reaching for something in her coat pocket.

'Excuse me.' He had something in his other hand – the one that wasn't touching Madge.

Peggy hoped Carole had one of her deadly knitting needles.

He was panting and out of breath and there was an agonising wait before he spoke. 'Sorry. You dropped your phone back there. I've been chasing you for ages, trying to give it back.'

Madge's face was blank as she accepted the proffered device.

'Thank you, young man,' said Peggy on Madge's behalf. It was a testament to Madge's state of mind that she allowed Peggy to speak for her.

The man braced himself with his hands on his knees, still breathing heavily. 'No worries. Just glad I caught you.' When he stood back upright, Peggy realised he was older than she'd first thought – probably in his fifties. 'Everything all right? Bit late for a stroll, innit?'

'We're fine,' said Peggy. 'Thank you for returning my friend's phone. That was very considerate.'

He nodded. 'No worries. Have a good night, then.'

Baz smiled, though it looked forced. 'You too. And thank you again.'

Five minutes later, the women rounded the final corner, turning onto Brookmill Road. When they got to the gate, Madge pulled Arthur's keys from her pocket. 'Now we just have to figure out which of these opens the lock.'

She tried three or four keys before finding the right one. All the while, Peggy was silently breathing the words 'hurry up hurry up hurry up'. She couldn't read lips, but she suspected Baz was whispering the same thing. The nature reserve was always locked and people tended not to notice it was there. But four women messing about with keys at the entrance could raise suspicions.

Peggy breathed a sigh of relief as the lock finally swung free. She steered her scooter in, taking care not to bump the trailer against the sides.

The site was hilly – too steep for her heavy load. She wedged the scooter into the corner next to the gate and disembarked. She left the trailer where it was for now. Old Arthur wasn't going anywhere.

The nature reserve had no lights of its own, but the street was brightly lit. Madge swung the gate shut, the hinges creaking abominably.

First things first: the women gloved up.

Peggy studied the map and tried to find the spot while Madge and Baz affixed a tarpaulin to the interior side of the gate to keep passersby from stopping to *help*.

So much for the reputation Londoners had for being cold and aloof.

Once Peggy had located the spot where Fifi's grave seemed to be, she beckoned the others over. She also bent down and stabbed a spike into the ground. The top was a simple cross. Peggy hung a photo of Fifi – helpfully downloaded from the internet – on the cross. That should make even the dullest-witted cop question what might be down there.

Peggy stood upright and put her hands to her hips, arching her back to stretch out sore, tired muscles. 'All right. I'm going to need some assistance here.' She walked back to the trailer and grabbed the hook on the back of the scooter where the trailer was affixed. Once they detached it from the scooter, it was like steering a wheelbarrow without handles – unwieldy.

Madge and Carole guided the trailer with its not-so-precious contents to the grave marker Peggy had added.

Peggy put a hand out to Madge. 'Gimme the keys.'

Madge looked up at her from her position, hunched over the heavily laden trailer. 'A little politeness is never uncalled for, you know.'

Peggy rolled her eyes. 'Give me the keys, please.'

'See? That didn't hurt.' Madge reached into her coat pocket and handed them over.

Peggy swiped the keys from her friend. 'Madge, it's late, it's cold, and I'm tired. May we dispense with the formalities, *please?*'

'It's never too late or too cold for good manners,' Madge replied. 'But after the night I've had, I understand your sentiment.'

A family of foxes emerged from somewhere. They stood at a distance and watched the women work, their eyes alight with curiosity.

Peggy and Baz headed for the tool shed. It took Peggy six

tries before she found the right key. When the lock slid open, Peggy unhooked it. An almighty creak pierced the night as the door swung open. The two women stepped into the darkness.

Baz was first to pull out her phone and shine the torch into the small space. 'Oh my word.'

Peggy inhaled sharply. 'That certainly makes our job easier.'

The toolshed was neatly organised. It seemed Arthur had wholeheartedly bought into the 'a place for everything and everything in its place' mentality. The side walls were covered in tools and implements. The workbenches were neat and free of detritus. Below the counters, the shelves were well organised, stacked with compost and whatever else. But the far wall...

'It's a shrine,' Baz whispered.

Peggy exhaled, her breath forming a cloud of vapour in front of her face. 'Yes, Baz. I can see that.'

Baz walked to the far wall and studied the display. She lifted a gloved hand and moved it around, like she was looking for something.

Newspaper reports on the disappearances were pinned next to photos and clips from the victims' social media pages. The wall was covered with pictures and papers. And between them were small personal items. A necklace hung over a photo of Hassan. A picture of Moses was partially obscured by a cheap digital watch. Two keys were taped to a photo of Wilson.

'What are you looking for?' Peggy was disgusted to find herself whispering too. The urge was overwhelming. She couldn't bring herself to speak at a normal volume in this unholy space.

Baz breathed slowly. 'Sign of anyone we don't already know about.' The torchlight caught the cloud formed by her words.

Peggy nodded. She directed her torch and joined Baz. 'I don't see anything unexpected. Well, not ... you know what I mean. So far I'm only seeing people – victims – we're already aware of.'

Baz held a finger out and touched a photo that hung on its own. 'Pius.'

Peggy squeezed Baz's shoulder. 'We should get what we came for and go back to the others.' They left the toolshed door wide open.

They found a shovel easily enough and returned to where Madge and Carole were arranging Arthur's body. He was lying on his back, in a pose one might expect a heart attack victim to be discovered in.

Madge took the shovel from Baz and pressed Arthur's fingers to various positions on it. 'His fingerprints are probably already on it. But it's best to be sure.'

She pressed the shovel into the earth and left it standing upright near Arthur's body. Next she removed a phone from her pocket and chucked it to the ground a little way away – far enough that he wouldn't have been able to reach it.

Madge dusted her gloved hands off. 'That's that part of the job done, I think.'

The others agreed, so they all set about gathering their stuff up. Peggy and Baz got back on their scooters. Carole pulled the tarpaulin down and folded it up. When they were finished, they looked at one another.

'Right, time to get ready for stage three.' Peggy steered her scooter back out onto the road.

———

ALL TOO SOON, Peggy's alarm was buzzing. Carole stirred but didn't wake as Peggy pulled herself out of bed. Cookie didn't even budge.

'What kind of ungodly time is this?' Peggy muttered as she flipped the light on in the bathroom.

A quarter of an hour later, Peggy locked the door behind her. Cookie waited patiently while she guided the mobility scooter out the front door. The sun wouldn't rise for another two hours at this time of year. Oh, how she loathed early morning starts.

Cookie hadn't been pleased about the wakeup either, but he wasn't about to let her go without him — which was just as well as the plan wouldn't have worked without him.

Peggy turned onto Vanguard Street and then a few moments later, she turned again onto Friendly Street. For his part, Cookie seemed less interested than usual in sniffing everything. Though he did stop to do his business right in front of the house where Peggy and her friends had done away with that troublesome lout the papers still insisted on calling the Goldsmiths Groper. Peggy chuckled to herself as she patted Cookie on the head. 'That's a good lad.'

For a moment as they approached the dog park, Cookie got excited. His tail fell slightly as they carried on past it. Eventually, they got to Lewisham Way and turned left.

In order to get to their destination from the other direction, they had to go the long way round. More than half an hour after leaving home, Peggy and Cookie arrived at the gates of the nature reserve. She stopped and turned off her mobility scooter. Once she had retrieved her phone from her pocket, she dialled 999.

'Hello. Police, fire, or ambulance, please?' The voice was far cheerier than anyone had any business being at six o'clock on a Saturday morning.

Peggy put on her best frightened-old-woman voice. 'Oh dear. I'm not sure. Probably police. Maybe ambulance. I suppose both, actually.' She threw a little quiver into her voice for maximum impact.

'Okay, love. I'll put you through to the police. They'll alert the paramedics if they think they're needed. Okay? Transferring you now.'

There were crackles and bleeps on the line and then a new voice. Gruffer. And significantly more Welsh. 'Good morning. You're through to the police. What seems to be the trouble?'

'Oh dear,' said Peggy, still playing the helpless crone. 'It's my dog, you see. He's found something and he won't leave it be. No, Cookie, no. Don't touch that.'

Cookie, who was snoozing on the pavement, looked up at the mention of his name. His ears perked and he cocked his head quizzically.

'All right, ma'am,' said the telephone operator. 'What is it you think he's found?'

'I was having trouble sleeping, you see. I often do. The GP gives me pills, only I don't like the way they make me feel, so I try not to take them. And often a good long walk does the trick instead. Anyhow, I woke up and couldn't drift off again, so I thought I'd go for a walk. It's lovely and clear out. No wind. No clouds. And we were having such a nice walk too. Only...' Peggy allowed her voice to trail off for a moment.

The call-centre cop, who clearly had the patience of a saint but who needed her to get to the point, said, 'Only then you found something that's given you a bit of a spook – am I right?'

'Yes, we were passing the Brookmill Nature reserve – do you know it?' Peggy asked.

'No, I'm afraid I don't, love. Now, what was it you found?'

'Oh, right. Yes, well, Cookie – he's my dog. A great big Alsatian. He weighed forty-two kilos at his last weigh-in. I don't know what that is in old money. When did they stop using stones – that's what I want to know.'

The officer on the phone cleared his throat.

'Oh, yes. Sorry. Anyhoo, when we got to the nature reserve on Brookmill Road, he started fussing at the gate, trying to get in like.' Cookie looked up at her as though he knew full well she was telling fibs about him. She'd have to get him an extra special treat later for his service. 'I tried to drag him onwards, but he just wasn't having it. I thought it was probably a fox. You know what London's like – foxes everywhere. But I shone my torch on the spot where he was focused – and you wouldn't believe it.'

'What was it?' Even this saintly cop/telephone operator was losing patience with her now. Good.

'A body!' Peggy practically squealed. 'A human body. I hope they're not dead – but then I suppose you have to ask why they'd be lying on the ground in the nature reserve if they're not?'

Now he was paying attention. 'Can you check whether they're breathing for me, love?'

'No, that's what I'm telling you,' said Peggy. 'He – or I suppose it could be she – is inside the nature reserve. I'm outside on Brookmill Road.'

'Okay,' he said. 'I'm sending police and an ambulance. While you wait for them, is it safe for you to go inside the park for me?'

Peggy did her best to sound indignant. 'I'm not climbing over that fence.'

'There must be a gate somewhere?'

'I told you already,' Peggy said. 'I'm standing at the gate.'

'Okay.' The coperator hadn't just lost patience. He seemed to have lost the thread. 'That's good. I want you and your dog – make sure you take your dog – to go into the park.' Were the people who worked in police call centres even cops?

'I already told you I'm not climbing the bloody fence, young man.' Peggy found herself making faces and gestures to accompany the role she was playing.

'Sorry. Why don't you try opening the gate?' She could picture him touching his fingers to his forehead, massaging his temples as he spoke.

'I don't have the key,' Peggy said.

'The key?' asked the maybe-cop.

'The key,' Peggy repeated as the sound of approaching sirens drowned out her words. 'Oh, there's the Old Bill now.'

'Okay, I'll let you go, then,' said the phone police. 'I hope your day improves from here on out.'

As the car pulled up, Peggy retrieved her secret weapon from her coat pocket: cheese. As soon as he got wind of it, Cookie sat up and paid attention, pawing at Peggy's hand. Before turning to face the officers, Peggy chucked a few cubes of cheddar through the slats in the gate in the direction of the corpse. That should help facilitate Cookie's role in this show.

As Peggy turned back around to see the two cops getting out of the car, her heart fell. Peter and Keeley. She'd have to abandon the role of vulnerable old bat. Peter would see through that in no time – and she suspected Keeley would too.

When Peter registered who it was, he picked up the pace, jogging towards her. 'Auntie? What happened? Are you okay?'

'Oh, Peter.' Peggy allowed a bit of her true self to seep into her performance. 'Thank heavens you're here. There's someone in the nature reserve – I think they're dead. Cookie's frantic.'

True to Peggy's words, Cookie was desperately scrabbling, trying to climb under the gate to get into the nature reserve. Give that boy a BAFTA.

CHAPTER 22

wherein normalcy resumes

DESPITE THE SUN, there was a chill to the air on this February morning. Baz shivered as she stepped into the warmth of Wellbeloved Café. The scents of coffee and chocolate and pastries filled her with pleasure. 'Morning, ladies.' She gave her friends a cheerful little wave as she stuck her head around the corner into the second room.

Only the ladies weren't there. Or rather, Madge was in her usual spot. But the people sitting in Peggy and Carole's chairs were not Peggy and Carole. Madge was deep in conversation with two people.

'Blue! Ron!' Baz felt like she hadn't seen the couple in ages; she was delighted by their presence. 'How are you both?'

Blue and Ron got out of their seats and made their way to Baz, enveloping her in the warmest of hugs. Ron held a teeny tiny dog in the crook of his arms. 'Don't mind Bunny – she loves a good cuddle.'

As they finally pulled away, Baz excused herself before they could say anything. 'I'll just go order my tea, shall I?'

When she returned a few minutes later, Blue and Ron

were hugging Peggy and Carole. Peggy backed out of their embrace and waved them off. In Ron's arms, Bunny was barking, growling, and snarling at Cookie. Cookie – whose nose was bigger than the entirety of Bunny – was cowering under the table.

Blue put her hands on her hips. 'Well, ducks. We just stopped by to thank you for everything you did for those poor people. I know you weren't able to help—'

Ron punched his partner playfully on the arm. 'Oh my days, Blue! These ladies did everything they could. It's not their fault the *Killer Queen* popped his clogs before he could be brought to justice.'

Peggy inhaled noisily as she dropped into her seat. 'Not you two using that awful moniker!'

She'd been railing against the name since the news of Arthur's crimes had hit international news several days ago. Baz wasn't even sure where the name had originated. When the news first broke, the press were calling Arthur the *Rainbow Ripper*. But twenty-four hours later, all that changed. News outlets latched onto the ridiculous – not to mention factually inaccurate – Killer Queen.

Ron raised his hand to stave off any more of Peggy's rant. 'Oh, I know. I know. I'm using it facetiously. Anyhow, we appreciate everything you tried to do. You worked hard to figure out what happened to Sue and all the others. It means a lot to us – to the whole community that you cared enough to try. Even though ... you know.'

Blue fanned herself. 'I suppose we'll have to take comfort in the fact that man will never lay a hand on anyone ever again.'

'Anyhow, lovies.' Still cradling Bunny in one arm, Ron took Blue by the elbow. 'We just wanted to come and thank you for everything you tried to do. I know the outcome wasn't what we'd all hoped – but at least it's over now.'

'The tickets,' exclaimed Blue, clearly refusing to be led away when she still had a mission.

Ron released Blue's arm. 'Oh, goodness me. I almost forgot. Go on, then. Tell them what they've won.'

Blue began rummaging through her pockets. 'We've, er, we've brought you free tickets for our next show. If you want to attend, that is. Of course, if you can't make that one or if you'd prefer a different show...'

Ron sighed and reached into his partner's coat pocket – one she'd already checked twice – and removed a folded sheet of paper.

'Cheers, m'dear,' said Blue. She unfolded the page and offered it to the women. She wasn't sure which woman to give it to, so she ended up sort of waving it between them.

After a moment, Peggy snatched the paper from Blue and read it. 'Thank you, Blue. Ron. That's lovely.' She looked at Madge and then Baz. 'Free tickets to Royal Tea's drag brunch at Buster Mantis. You know, the Jamaican place down in the Arches.'

Ron nodded. 'It's this coming Saturday. Though, as I say, if you'd prefer a different show, just let us know.'

'You're always welcome at any of our shows,' Blue said before raising an index finger. 'But one freebie and then you've got to buy a ticket like everyone else. After all, a girl's got to eat.'

Warmth spread through Baz's body – the pleasant sort, though, not the embarrassment she so often felt. 'I can't speak for my friends, but I can think of nothing I'd rather do.'

Blue squeezed Baz's shoulder. 'Cheers, love.'

'We'll all be there,' said Peggy.

Blue and Ron turned to leave, with Bunny casting a final few snarls from the safety of Ron's arm. In the archway through to the next room, they almost crashed into Sarah.

Once the drinks were distributed and all the associated pleasantries exchanged, the women settled down to focus on their crafts – and their chat.

Baz removed her embroidery from her bag. 'I heard from my solicitor yesterday afternoon.'

'Oh?' Peggy's eyes were still focused on her computer.

Madge peered over the top of her glasses. 'The one from Chuk's firm?'

Baz nodded. 'Everything's all nice and official now. Contracts have been exchanged. I'll get the keys just over two weeks from now.'

Peggy winked. 'See? Sometimes a little crime does pay.'

Madge sucked at her teeth and waved a dismissive hand at Peggy. 'Well done, Baz.'

'I'm going to go and have a chat with Debs once I leave here,' Baz said. 'I had a look through all the contracts and everything. I'll be able to do the work the building needs and still reduce the rent.'

Peggy finally looked up from her computer. 'Good for you.'

A companionable silence fell over the group for a few moments – even the café was quieter than normal. It was only because it was so quiet that Baz heard a tiny ping from the direction of Peggy's computer. She clicked a few keys and then her eyes widened.

'Oh, ho ho!' Peggy pinched her lips together like she was stifling a chuckle. 'I had an alert set up. You'll never guess what the council's just announced.'

Madge made a rolling *go on* gesture with one of her knitting needles, fine ombre pink wool billowing in the air after it.

'The developer has backed out of the deal to buy the nature reserve. Subsequently, the council announced their intention to "rethink" their plans.' Peggy made rabbit ears around the relevant word.

Madge turned to Baz. 'Oh, I keep meaning to ask you, Baz. Have you heard any more from this friend of yours – Paul?'

Baz winced as she stabbed herself with her embroidery needle. A teensy speck of blood welled up. 'I, erm, that is...'

Peggy looked up from her laptop. 'He seemed quite keen on you, didn't he?'

Madge shook her head and offered Baz a tissue from her pocket. 'You really ought to get yourself a thimble.'

Baz inhaled slowly, willing the heat from spreading to her cheeks. 'I'm going to be seeing Paul this evening, actually. He's coming to mine for dinner.'

Peggy and Madge swapped glances, grimacing.

Baz raised a hand to stave off their comments. 'Daisy's going to help me with the cooking. That is, I say help. But we all know she'll end up doing most of the work.'

Peggy nodded. 'That's probably for the best.'

Baz begrudgingly agreed. The women shared a split second of silence before it was broken by the bell over the front door. A soft tenor voice called out, 'Yoo-hoo! Wagwan, ladies?'

Clive was followed by the giant of a man that was Chuk Ibeh. Cookie pulled himself out from under the table and danced in circles around Chuk.

Chuk was wearing that scrumptious cologne again. The man smelt positively heavenly, with notes of apple and musk and cedar.

'Morning, Mags. Ladies.' He bent to give Madge a quick hug.

'Good to see you, Chukwuma.' Madge looked up from her knitting.

Chuk looked down at Cookie – which was all it took to get Cookie to sit. His enormous tail swished back and forth, tickling Baz's ankles each time it came her way. 'Hello, Cookie. Will you give me a paw?'

Cookie practically punched Chuk's thigh in his enthusiasm. Chuk took the paw and shook it. 'Good boy. Now let's see if I've got anything for you here.' Cookie nosed one of Chuk's pockets before the man could even look inside. He pushed the dog's nose away gently and retrieved a bag of treats from the pocket.

Cookie stood up, twirled around, then sat back down, before batting at Chuk with one paw and then the other.

Chuk's laugh was a booming, uproarious sound. 'That's a good boy. Here you go.' He allowed Cookie to snaffle treats from his hand.

Once that was done, Clive pushed his way past Chuk. 'You'll never guess what!'

Peggy heaved a sigh. 'All well, I trust, Chuk?'

'It is indeed,' replied Chuk. 'I came this way this morning to meet with my client to deliver some good news.' Chuk waved at Clive. 'And he suggested we stop by to see you ladies.'

'Madge and her friends were investigating the people who went missing,' said Clive. 'Especially my friend Eddie. You probably read about it in the papers – it's been all over the news lately. The Rainbow Ripper – I won't mention the other name the papers have been calling him. My friend Eddie was one of his victims. Anyway, the ladies tried to find him. Although they didn't do anything in the end. In fact, the Rainbow Ripper died before anyone found out what he was doing.'

Clive stilled for a moment before turning to the women. 'Still, it's nice you tried.'

Madge frowned.

Peggy rolled her eyes. 'What do you want, Clive?'

Clive clapped. 'Oh, I just came to say thank you for suggesting that the deliciously beefy Chuk help me with my immigration issues. He put my application together and says I have a really good case. He came to tell me this morning that I've got a court date. It's not until April, but I suppose at least it's good to know the wheels are in motion.'

Madge lifted a single eyebrow. 'Good for you, Clive.'

'Anyhow, that's all.' Clive bent to get a closer look at Madge's knitting.

He reached out to finger the wool but she slapped him away. 'It's been nice seeing you, Clive.'

Peggy made a shooing motion.

'Fine.' Clive shook his head. 'A lady can tell when she's not wanted.' He fondled Chuk's coat, running his fingers down the lapel. 'And I'll see you in April. Of course, if you want to see me before then, you only have to call.' He tapped a nail against the taller man's chest before mincing out of the shop.

Madge shook her head. 'What an odious little man.'

Chuk threw back his head and released a surprisingly delicate laugh. 'Clive? A little odd perhaps, but he's actually quite sweet.'

Peggy and Madge both harrumphed.

Chuk wagged a finger at Madge. 'And he's certainly got a soft spot for you.' He pulled another treat from his pocket then bent down to give it to Cookie. When he stood back up, he smoothed his trousers. 'I best be off.'

'Give my regards to Laura,' said Madge.

'I will, Mags. You should come round for dinner one day. Maybe you could bring Clive.' Chuk winked at Baz while Madge flustered and spluttered.

He waved at the women before ducking through to the café's main room. He called his greetings to Sarah before heading out into the morning sun.

When the door fell shut behind him, Madge shook her head. 'Sometimes I can't believe I married that man.'

Baz coughed up the tea she'd just drunk. 'I'm sorry – you what?'

Madge's eyes shifted left and right. 'Chuk and I—'

Baz furrowed her brow. 'Yes?'

Madge looked Baz right in the eye. 'We used to be married.'

Baz had to remind herself to breathe. 'You what?'

Madge cocked her head and looked at Baz. 'Surely you heard Peter call him Grandad?'

It was unnaturally warm in the café, Baz was sure of it. 'Yes, but most people have four grandparents. I assumed you were connected by marriage. That is, by someone else's marriage.' She shook her head. 'Hang on, no, that doesn't make sense. You were showing one another pictures of your great-grandchildren. If you two used to be married, wouldn't they be his great-grandchildren too?'

Madge laughed. 'Baz, I'm so glad you joined our little group. You are such a joy.' Madge set back to work on her knitting. 'Chuk and I have two kids together: Tony and Em. And we share five grandkids – including Peter – and one great-grandbaby. Tiana was my second and his first. She'll be three in a few weeks.'

Carole looked up and grinned. 'The truth is ... alligators are much better suited to playing the accordion.' Then she laughed so hard she had to stomp her feet on the floor a bit.

Baz leant back in her chair and returned her focus to her embroidery work. 'I'm glad I joined you too.'

THANK you for reading my little book. I hope you enjoyed it.

If you're not already on my email list, you can join it now and get a free story.

Click the image to download Friends in Need for free

the end (for now)

Thank you for reading *All Tea, No Shade, and a Bit of Murder*, the second novel in the *Vigilauntie Justice series*.

My success or failure as an indie author depends largely on word-of-mouth recommendations. If you enjoyed this book, please consider leaving a review. And honestly, if you despised this book with the very fibre of your soul ... **please leave a review**.

Baz, Peggy, Carole, and Madge will almost certainly continue their mission to keep south-east London safe.

acknowledgements

First, last, and always... Thank you for reading.

I keep seeing posts in various writers' and readers' groups saying that writers shouldn't get political in their novels.

Bollocks to that.

Everything is politics. Everything.

Governments all over the world are oppressing people for who they are, who they love, how they express themselves, where they were born, the colour of their skin, their religion ... and for having the audacity to live as their authentic selves. To remain neutral is to side with the oppressor.

Anyways...

I owe a huge thank you to That Girl for lifting the metaphorical curtain to give me a sneaky little peek into what goes on behind the scenes in drag. She patiently responded to my ridiculous questions and listened to all my absurd theorising. I hope her input has lent an air of authenticity to Blue, Di, Pfeff, and Coco. If not ... well, that's on me. I swear I had the very best teacher.

As always, the WiFi Sci-Fi writers' group has been the most amazing gift. They continually teach, push, and cheerlead me to be a better writer.

I want to thank my beta readers: Julie Golden and Stephanie Francis. They both got stuck right into the guts of my ridiculous tale and helped provide a buff and polish.

Nick and Hannah, my editors, dug into the meat of this

vegetarian story to make it the best version of itself it could be. Any mistakes you find now are entirely my own fault.

Finally, my legally contracted lifemate, Dave, has been putting up with more than any human being should have to. If you've ever met me in real life, you'll understand what a big deal that is. Seriously ... I'm *a lot*. Dave has listened to me talk about my imaginary friends every single day for six years. Dave's the best person.